SPIRIT OBSESSED

BRENDA BENGTSON

ISBN: 978-1-7375017-0-1 (paperback) - ISBN: 978-1-7375017-1-8 (eBook)

www.brendabengtson.com

Editor: Rachel Garber

Cover design: Marijke van Leeuwen at www.cutting-edge-studio.com

The World English Bible (WEB) is a Public
Domain (no copyright) Modern English translation of the Holy Bible. That means that you may freely copy it in any form including electronic and print formats.

DEDICATION

To my husband, Bob, and our children Tyler, Haley, Tanner, and Hunter thank you for taking this journey with me and believing in my story.

CAN YOU HELP?

"Thank You For Reading My Grandma's Book!"

Dear Reader:

Please leave me an honest review wherever you purchased this book.

Thank you for reading **SPIRIT OBSESSED.**

Brenda Bengtson

www.brendabengtson.com

"Even though I walk through the valley of the shadow of death, I will fear no evil, for you are with me"

Psalm 23:4 WEB

CHAPTER ONE

I laid down in my bed, afraid to fall asleep, and gulped down my breaths to stay quiet. I knew if I closed my eyes, my dream would come back to haunt me as it had done so many times before. What was once a childhood dream had evolved into a nightmare. My dream left me surrounded by evil darkness and no way to escape. At night, the doorway of our darkened bedroom caused fear in my mind. It was the entryway where evil would come and seize me. Would this dream ever go away?

Two years ago, Brock insisted I see a doctor about my nightmares. At first, I was hesitant, but I could see the worried look in his eyes as he hugged me tight into his body and said, "Remi, I don't want you to be afraid to go to sleep anymore." The next day I called the sleep doctor who I knew from having worked as a nurse in the hospital, had a sleep study done a week later, and confirmed I had a problem with sleep talking and night terrors. The doctor informed me that only five percent of children carry this diagnosis into adulthood. There was no specific treatment. I refused anxiety medication since I enjoyed my red wine in the evenings, stayed away from horror movies, got a lavender plug-in for the bedroom, kept my usual bedtime routine, and tried to write my thoughts in a journal. These were only temporary fixes to a permanent problem that would not leave.

I glanced over at the window and could see the streetlight's glow as it peeked through the curtains. I tucked my bed covers in tight around me while I laid my arms crossed upon my chest like a mummy in a coffin. Brock was right next to me as he snored loudly and caused the bed to have a slight vibration.

Suddenly, my eyes became heavy like dead weights that pressed onto my lids and forced them closed. I resisted and kept my eyes opened. It was a losing battle. Complete darkness surrounded me and a deathly quiet was all around.

"No, no, no, get me out of here! He's going to kill me! I don't want to die!" I shouted. But no one was around to hear my cries of fear and desperation to escape the darkness that had a hold over me. Just when I thought it would swallow me whole, the darkness parted. I saw daylight as if heaven had opened up and shined its light down on me. Immediately, my leg muscles tightened as I took off and ran frantically through a field of tall weeds that consumed my body. I could sense that I was not alone, wherever this place might be. There was someone out there who watched my every move, which made my stomach churn and my body quiver from fear of the unknown. Nothing around me looked familiar. There was no place to go for safety. No matter how far or fast I ran, the evil darkness would eventually catch up with me. What had I done to make this thing hunt me down like a wild animal? As I continued to run, my feet pounded on the hard, uneven ground, which caused my arms to swing swiftly in rhythm with the steps. I clenched my mouth tight to stop the jarring vibration of my teeth. Every beat of my heart pumped faster than my legs could run. My nostrils flared open as I tried to take in more oxygen. I ran as if my life depended on it. Whatever was out there had a powerful force that tried to pull me backward, as if I were a piece of steel drawn to a magnet. Where was I? The prickly leaves and stems from the weeds scratched every part of my exposed skin as I used my bare hands to push them away. I felt a stinging sensation and saw tiny droplets of blood that oozed from the freshly opened cuts. How had I ended up in this place? Was this a dream? Everything around me seemed so real. While I ran, each breath I inhaled and exhaled caused a slow burning pain deep in my throat that made me choke. What was my purpose for being in this field?

My vision became hindered by the bright sun in the noonday sky. The air was hot and sticky. Beads of sweat built up from every part of my body. My hair stuck to my neck and face. I took the back of my hand and swept it across my forehead as I removed the perspiration that dripped down onto my eyelashes. My skin turned red as it burned in the intense heat.

I looked up with widened eyes and an opened mouth as the darkness came back and loomed over my head. An image of a large, evil, devilish beast flashed into my mind. I continued to run, even though my strength faded and my body felt limp with exhaustion. Fear caused me to tremble at what was out there and that it would take away my life. Where would my final destination lead me? Would I be safe?

I stopped and bent over as I gasped for air to catch my breath. My heart pounded fast in my chest, as if it would explode. I stood back up and looked around as I noticed the tall weeds were no longer there. My body froze mid-movement at the edge of a rocky cliff that led to a dark abyss. If I took one more step, the fall would lure me to my death.

Just then, I drew my eyes to the left, where I saw lush green trees in the distance along a mountainous hillside. In front of the hillside was a flat piece of barren land. It was a stark contrast between the living and the dead. As I turned toward the right, my eyes caught sight of an outline that appeared to be a man who wore gray clothing as he sat on the ground. It was hard to focus up close as my vision became blurred from lack of hydration while I ran in the scorching sun. I had a sense that this man was not the one who chased after me, but I couldn't recognize who it might be. What was this person doing?

Beside the man, I could see rocky clay soil around a large, deep, rectangular hole that resembled a grave that had been dug recently in the barren ground. The man had dirt that covered his face, hands, and clothing. Had he dug the hole? There was no shovel. What was the reason for this hole in the ground? All at once, I noticed that the man had stood up and looked at me, or maybe he looked through me. I couldn't tell. He was taller than me, but I wasn't afraid of him. Why? The man reached out his arm and pointed to something behind me. Slowly, I turned, and the darkness came back and overpowered me, which caused the sun to be obscured. There was a feeling of dread and doom that came over me. My voice shook and my body trembled as I asked, "Who's out there? What do you want from me? Leave me alone!" There was no response inside the darkness.

The darkness waited for me until I arrived at this cliff. It drew closer to where I stood and had no shape. A toxic odor wafted through the air, similar to a wild animal that decayed in the woods, which caused me to have fast, shallow breaths and turned my skin bluish-gray. It felt like the veil of darkness grabbed at my throat, which suffocated me and paralyzed my body. My arms and legs weakened as I fell backwards at the cliff's edge. I knew I would die as I screamed out, "God save me!" Then, I woke up.

"Remi, Remi, are you okay?" asked Brock, as he sat up and reached for my arm with his strong yet gentle touch. I leaned forward in bed to catch my breath. Excess perspiration from my body made the sheets feel cold against my skin. I could hear Brock saying my name as I snapped back to reality. The smell of his spice cologne comforted me as it still clung to his body from the previous morning. As I looked over at Brock, his ruffled hair was on one side of his head. He hadn't changed his position while he slept.

"What was I doing?" I asked, as I pulled back the dampened covers.

"You must have had one of your nightmares again. This time you were screaming out to God. Are you okay?" asked Brock, as he reached over to pull me close to him.

"This dream felt real unlike the ones I've had before."

"What made it feel real?"

"It felt like I was dying. This darkness kept chasing me, and I was falling off a cliff to my death. That must have been when I woke up."

"I'm sorry your dream scared you. If I could take your dream away, I would in a heartbeat. All I can do right now is just hold you."

"Just being here after my dream is enough," I said as I held out my trembling hands and forced them into a fist to make it stop. "Go back to sleep, Brock. I'll be okay."

"Boy Scout promise?" Brock asked, holding up three fingers.

"You keep forgetting I was in Girl Scouts, and yes, I promise," I said, holding up three fingers. We both smiled at each other as Brock leaned in to kiss me and lay back down to sleep.

I had said the words that I was okay, but my mind and body felt differently. There was nothing Brock could do to help me, except be here. It was my nightmare, and it always would be.

My legs felt weak when I got out of bed and walked to the bathroom. I stood at the sink, splashed cold water on my face, and used the soft hand towel afterward, which felt soothing against my skin. As I looked in the mirror, my face was pale as a ghost. I leaned over to drink water from the spigot and rehydrated my body. My mind went back to my dream and how it shook me to my core. When I walked out of the bathroom, I headed to the dresser for some clean clothes. I tossed my dirty clothes in the hamper and walked over to my favorite oversized chair that sat in the room's corner and picked up the folded quilt that was laying over it. The chair and quilt were Grandma Leona's that I had inherited when she passed. As a child, I sat in that chair in front of her fireplace and covered myself with her quilt that she had pieced together. It always made me feel comforted, wrapped up in its warmth.

When I came back to bed with the quilt, Brock was lying on his right side with his head on the pillow, sound asleep as he snored. This was his favorite position when he wanted to fall asleep fast and it helped eliminate noise distractions. A childhood baseball injury to his head made him deaf in his left ear. He looked so peaceful when he slept. When he snored, I felt safe and comforted with him by my side. I was not alone whenever my fears from my dream tried to overpower my mind. If only I could fall asleep that fast. I glanced over at the clock on the bedside table. It was a few minutes after three o'clock in the morning.

There was something different that occurred in my dream tonight than in the ones I had in the past. Usually, I stood at a distance in my dream as I observed everything around me. This time I was inside the dream and interacted with whoever was out there. The physical and emotional pain felt real. Had this dark, evil beast wanted something from me? Who was the man by the hole in the ground? Was this a premonition of my death to come? I had a bad feeling my dream would lead me straight to its reality and one day I would see this beast face-to-face.

I crawled back into bed and felt my sheets were still damp. I flipped over my pillow, settled down on top of the covers, and pulled the quilt over me to my chin to stay warm.

There were only a couple hours left before the alarm would go off and our day would begin. While I was lying in bed, I had a hard time closing my eyes. Why was I having this same dream? Each time it occurred, there were bits and pieces that changed. Where was this place located? Little by little my dream faded away from the man in the gray clothing and focused on my demise. My vision became blurred in my dream, and it was hard to recognize what was in front of me. This time, all I could see at the end of my dream was a heavy darkness. What was the meaning behind my dream?

The questions lingered in my mind as I forced my eyes closed and tried to go back to sleep. The kids would be up soon, and I needed to rest some more before the day began. I wouldn't have time to decipher my dream right now or focus on what my demise might be. I needed sleep. As I closed my eyes, I could see myself at

Grandma Leona's in front of the fireplace as I sat in her favorite chair, hugged her quilt closer to me, and drifted off to sleep.

All at once, I startled awake and looked at the clock. I realized I had slept through the alarm. I must have missed the snooze button and hit the off button on the alarm instead. It was six-thirty and still dark outside.

"Oh no, the kids are going to be late for the school bus!" I said in a panic. Immediately, I jumped out of bed and yelled down the hallway, "Come on, kids! Get up. You're going to be late for school." I ran into the bathroom and took a super quick shower. The water didn't have time to get warm. Afterward, I stood on the bath mat, looked in the mirror, and said my mantra aloud, "You can do this, Remi, just breathe." There was no time to put on my make-up or blow dry my hair. I hurriedly got dressed and remarked under my breath, "Wow, five minutes. That's a record."

It was March 2019 and another hectic Monday morning in the Sterling family household . . . same routine . . . different day. Three of our four children were in school. Our oldest son, Dex, acted older than his young ten years as he charmed all the girls at school with his blonde hair and light blue eyes. He enjoyed art and had a passion to one day make it a living. Londyn was our eight-year-old brown hair, brown-eyed princess. Her entrepreneur skills led to deals with the neighbors for snow shoveling, leaf raking, and lemonade drink sales, with dreams of owning her own business one day. Nox loved bugs and animals, and at seven with his dark brown hair and dark brown eyes, he knew animal science would be his thing.

Each of the kids hurriedly followed me downstairs for their breakfast. I popped frozen pancakes in the microwave, Dex poured each a glass of milk, I handed Londyn the pancakes and she slapped some butter on them, and Nox got the syrup from the cabinet and silverware from the drawer. They gobbled down their food, ran back upstairs to brush their teeth, got their book bags, headed out the door, and jumped on the school bus at exactly seven o'clock.

"Okay, I took care of the first three. Now I have one more kid, a dog, and a husband left," I remarked under my breath rushing back inside the house.

I ran upstairs, helped three-year-old Max get dressed, and downstairs to the kitchen for breakfast. Max was our youngest child with blonde hair and blue-green eyes, just like mine. He had a love for playing tiny-tots basketball or whiffle ball and learned his moves from the pros on television. When Max was born, Brock and I decided it would be best to put my nursing career on hold until he started pre-school, then I would go back to work part-time. We had not planned for any more children, so I was glad to have this time with him. As Max pulled out his chair and sat down at the table, I looked over and noticed his hair stuck straight up on one side of his head. I smiled and thought, like father, like son.

Our German Shepherd, King, followed at my heels and expected his breakfast next. "I know, boy. I'll get your food, too," I said, as I refilled his dish. I gave King a pat on the head. "Here you go. Eat your breakfast." King inhaled his food like there was no tomorrow and lapped up his water like he had been in a desert for months. "Goodness King, slow down or you'll throw it back up," I said as I watched him closely.

After he ate, King lay down on the rug in the kitchen to rest. "It must be exhausting to be a dog." King looked at me as he tilted his head, hung out his tongue, and panted.

At the kitchen counter, I took a minute to get what I needed to fix a cup of coffee. I quickly scanned the cabinet, which showed the tin coffee container hid in the upper left corner. As I peeked inside, I saw there was barely any left. I glanced over at the refrigerator and saw my reminder note from yesterday to buy more coffee. I rolled my eyes and groaned as I realized how I always seemed to ignore my own notes in the mad rush of our active household. Maybe I should've put the note on my phone. Later today, I would need to make a trip to the grocery store. I scraped the bottom of the tin container for every coffee ground and hoped it would be enough.

The aroma of the freshly brewed coffee filled the air. If I could trap it in a bottle, I would take a sniff whenever I felt anxious. I poured the dark, rich coffee into my mug, sat down at the kitchen table with Max, and savored every sip. The caffeine kicked my brain into gear to jump start my day.

Brock was up and started getting ready for work. I fixed him a healthy breakfast, so he wouldn't raid the school vending machine and stock up on peanut butter chocolate wafer bars. He always had a weakness for these and would have two extra in his coat pocket whenever he came home from work. It may not have been the best snack choice, but Brock said it tasted so good.

Brock and I began our married life together as the Sterling's in June 2003. We made our home in Millburg, Virginia. It was a fast-paced college city. The energy from the twenty-something crowd kept us feeling young. Brock worked at Shepherds University as a Professor of Landscape Architect while I worked at the Children's Hospital as a pediatric nurse.

When Brock and I made our decision to start a family, we had four babies in seven years. The demand for a bigger home became inevitable. We looked around for a year before we found our current home that was the right fit for our family.

Today would be a busy workday at the college for Brock. He was the sole breadwinner of our family. Brock was my super stud with his dark brown hair, chocolate eyes, closely trimmed goatee, and sexy smile. He looked good, dressed up in a suit and tie for work with a hint of spice cologne. After work, he dressed down in his torn blue jeans, flannel shirt, and backward ball cap to do odd jobs around the house. He always got a few grease splatters on his hands and face along the way. No matter which way Brock dressed or looked, he rocked my world.

Brock headed to go out the side door to the garage, ready to face a full day of meetings and classes, when he pivoted midway and walked back over to the kitchen table where Max and I sat. He looked at me and said, "I forgot to tell you something yesterday."

"What did you forget to tell me?" I asked, puzzled.

"I finally got my transfer to Jamestown University approved. They're going to offer me better pay and benefits, plus I can transition to department head after working there for a year. If I stay at Shepherds, I would need to work five more years for the same opportunity."

My heart sunk at Brock's words. "Already? I know we talked about this, but I didn't think it would happen so soon. And how did you forget until now to tell me when you knew about this last night?"

"I did try to tell you about the job last night after the kids went to bed. But you said you were too tired to talk and could it wait until the morning. You looked exhausted. Your dreams are wearing you down. You really should see the sleep doctor again for a check-up."

"My mind must have wandered off when we talked last night. I forgot that part of the conversation. I've been faithfully following what the sleep doctor said after my study. I'm not sure what else he could recommend."

"You were physically drained last night when we went to bed. I held you close, and you finally relaxed. I knew you needed your rest. That's why I'm telling you about the job now. By the way, are you feeling better after that bad dream you had earlier this morning?"

"I'm feeling okay right now. I'm glad you held me last night and this morning. It makes me feel protected."

I thought, was I really okay? This same dream occurred in different variations for so long now my brain felt numb from it. I took a sip of my coffee and grimaced at the cold taste. The microwave was behind me as I walked over to reheat what I left in my cup and went back to the kitchen table and sat down with Max.

"So, Shepherds wasn't willing to increase your salary to keep you on staff?"

"I spoke with my boss about salary changes, but there wasn't any room for negotiation. We can't live on one salary at my current pay. We've already talked about this. You knew I was leaning towards accepting the Jamestown offer. We'll need to move to Cedarville by July, before fall semester starts."

"July? That's not a lot of time."

"I know. I need to get my classes set up by the first of August. The students come back to college two weeks later."

I said my mantra in my mind, "You can do this, Remi, just breathe," as I took a deep breath in and slowly let it out. "I'll call Raheem at the realty office today and tell him the news. He'll think we're crazy moving again."

Brock gave Max a kiss on the forehead. Then he reached over and gave me a hug and kiss. He assured me this move would be the best thing for our family. I hoped he would be right.

Immediately, I called Raheem and told him that Brock accepted a job in Cedarville, and our family needed to move by July.

"That's cutting it pretty close. We have four months to get you out of one house and into another one," Raheem reported with a sense of urgency in his voice.

"I know, Raheem. Do you think you could help us locate a house in Cedarville? Something with a bit of land, a house large enough for our family, and close enough to the school. If it needs some fixing up since we're on a deadline for moving, we would consider that option."

"Thank you for trusting me with that responsibility. I'll contact Ayesha Taylor. She's a realtor in Cedarville and a friend of mine. We'll work together to find a home. I'll be back in touch soon."

As I hung up the phone, I realized we would move from the home our family had grown to love. The kids would miss their friends in the neighborhood and classmates at school. I understood Brock's decision in changing jobs. He always looked out for our family's best interest. But in the back of my mind, I wondered why this had to happen? What would our life be like in Cedarville and what memories would we make there with our family? I guess we were about to find out.

CHAPTER TWO

The official moving day arrived for the Sterling household during the hottest July on record. The university arranged for professional movers to transport all of our belongings from Millburg to our new home six hours away in Cedarville. To prepare for our move, they packed the items from our home and into the moving truck the day before. Our family stayed overnight in a motel that allowed dogs, and today at seven o'clock we were ready to hit the road. I loaded up the kids and King in the van while Brock drove his own car. The movers set out ahead of us and we would meet in Cedarville at one of the local fast-food places for a late lunch, then on to the house.

The drive to Cedarville was uneventful. The kids entertained themselves as they watched a video on the pull-down screen in the van and fell asleep before it ended. King sat in the center of the backseat as he used Dex's lap for a pillow.

This was our first time in Cedarville as a family. Brock had been here when he came for his job interview at the university. He limited his time, but he walked downtown, took pictures of the area, and shared them with me. At that point, the job wasn't his yet. Once it was official, Brock came back to Cedarville and followed up with the realtor to see our new house, and took a few photos. During his visit, Brock mentioned there were some items to fix up, with the lights being one item, but the bones of the house were great. At one point during his visit, Brock mentioned that he heard what sounded like footsteps upstairs. He thought it was just his imagination, since he and the realtor were both downstairs and the only ones in the house. He chalked it up to the house being old and that sometimes a creaky sound just happens. I trusted Brock was right in his assumption about the sound he heard. Since it wasn't bothersome to him, I chose not to dwell on it either.

As we drove slowly through town, I rolled down my driver's side window. The atmosphere was one of a quaint college town with a population of 50,000 when students were on campus. There were Bradford Pear trees that lined the sidewalks on either side of the street. The two-lane road to the downtown area had your basic mom and pop shops and a mix of local and commercial type restaurants. When I stopped at the light, I could smell a variety of savory food aromas in the sultry summer air. There was a farmer's market stand on one side of the street with fresh vegetables, fruits, and handmade items being sold. The atmosphere was calm and relaxing: a far cry from the hustle and bustle that would exist when the students came back to campus.

We stopped at our pre-determined lunch spot in town for a quick bite to eat. The movers had arrived before us. We ate outside on the patio tables, and King joined us.

"I think we're going to like it here." I looked around, taking in the small town atmosphere.

"I certainly hope so. I'm tired of moving." Brock teased with a wink and a smile.

"It's almost like Millburg, but not as big."

"I think it's going to be perfect for our kids growing up here and for us when we're old enough to retire."

"Us grow old? Never," I teased back, giving Brock a hug.

We finished our lunch and everyone was excited to see our new home and get settled. It would be a twenty-minute drive from downtown. The movers left ahead of us and would unload the furniture as soon as we pulled into the driveway.

The two-lane road led us straight into the neighborhood where we would reach our ultimate destination. The homes in this area appeared to be showing their age through the years with overgrowth and peeled paint. There were no tree-lined streets or sidewalks like we had in Millburg. The area comprised farmland with barbed wire fences along the road's edge. The land behind the fence had large, older homes where families could raise farm animals and crops. As we drove by, I could see the leaves of the cornstalks in the fields as they bent in the wind. I had noticed no children playing outside in the yards of these homes. Maybe they were inside canning jars of food from their crops. The children may have already grown up while the parents lived in these houses and managed the farm. Some of these families must have been the ones who sold their produce downtown at the farmer's market.

Finally, up ahead on the left was the house we had purchased at 119 Westview Lane. It sat on a four acre lot in a remote location back from the main road on a hillside. It was a smaller lot than the ones we had noticed on the drive down and the last house on this side of the road.

When we approached the driveway entrance, it led to a straight dirt and gravel road that kicked up dust at the vehicle's wheels. At a distance, the house exuded a stately Colonial Williamsburg vibe and had more overgrowth on the surrounding land. The closer we got to the house; its age became more apparent. There was an ominous cloud hovered over it which looked similar to what we had seen in the realtor's picture. That's odd, I thought. This was my first time on the property, but it felt like I had been here before.

When Brock and I looked for our home in Cedarville, Ayesha had sent Raheem pictures of houses for us to choose. We wanted to make sure the house had enough land for the kids to play outside, as well as King, and enough space inside the house to accommodate our sizeable family. When Brock and I saw the Westview Lane picture, it drew us to its charm and character even though the weeds and ivy appeared to be taking over. Even the dark mist that hovered over the house on what appeared to be an overcast day couldn't take away the beauty of this older home. We could see the potential in bringing this house back to life after it had been unoccupied for so many years, and we would take on the challenge.

Raheem sold our home in Millburg after four weeks on the market. Several people came by to look, but only one buyer was interested. After much negotiation, we accepted the buyer's offer even though it was less than the asking price. We didn't want to risk paying for two mortgages going forward. Our family was ready to start a new chapter in a new town, and we hoped the transition would go smoothly.

The movers had arrived at our house first, while Brock and I pulled our vehicles directly behind them.

I walked over to Brock, puzzled, and asked, "Did you notice the dark mist in the sky?"

"Yes, I did. It looks just like the picture Ayesha sent to Raheem," recalled Brock. "Maybe it's just a cloud passing by. I don't believe there's any rain in the forecast."

"Don't you think it's strange that this dark mist was in the picture and now it's here on the day we move in? Does it come with the house?" I joked.

Brock chuckled. "That's a good one, Remi. I think it's a coincidence. I don't think it means anything bad. Let's get moved in. Maybe it'll leave soon." Brock reached over and gave me a hug.

Ayesha pulled up in the driveway and brought the keys to the house. When she stepped out of her car, she had this classy style. Her braided hair was impeccable, like an elegant piece of artwork. The sleeveless dress she wore looked like summer in shades of lemon and lime. The smell of her citrus perfume hung in the air. It was a perfect choice on this balmy day. The wedges on her sandals gave her short frame the height she needed to be eye to eye with her client.

After we exchanged pleasantries, Ayesha handed us a lovely gift basket filled with wine, a variety of cheeses, and crackers. She even threw in a bag of chocolate candy for the kids and a dog bone for King. She arranged for a house cleaning crew to come to the home earlier this week to prepare for our arrival. The lawn service crew could not make it because of a scheduling conflict. Ayesha had her husband use his weed trimmer and mower to remove some of the tall grass only in the front yard area and perimeter. She commented that her husband would have needed a hazmat suit to handle the tall prickly weeds in the backyard. She offered to reschedule the lawn service, and Brock let out a sigh of relief for the extra help.

"Check the outdoor electric outlet. My husband felt a little shock when he plugged up his weed trimmer. The house inspector didn't have it written on his list as a problem," said Ayesha with a look of concern on her face. "Also, he mentioned that there was a dark stain or something like that in the upstairs center window. I told him it may have been a shadow of a tree. Nothing is there now," said Ayesha as she looked up and pointed in that direction.

Brock jotted down both items on his phone and would follow-up. The movers waited a few minutes for Brock to look inside the house so he could direct them on where to place the furniture.

Before we moved to Cedarville, the home inspector had made a list of recommended updates. The last time anyone lived here was in 1999. Ayesha kept in touch with us and helped arrange services to have the central air unit replaced as it ignited a spark when it turned on and had stopped working. There were some issues with lights that flickered in the house, but the electrician couldn't find any defects with the wiring. The gas furnace was in good working order, although he heard an occasional clanging sound which could require follow-up if it persisted. Since we lived close to the town limits, there was water and sewer hook-up available and no odors or leaks detected. Appliances in the kitchen needed to be replaced since burners on the stove weren't working and the refrigerator wouldn't cool. Due to age, the roof might need replacement in the next five years. This 1940s house was well built without any foundation issues. The inspector commented to Ayesha, and she shared with us, that whoever built the house meant for it to stay there forever.

As I looked around, the house had a touch of Southern Colonial historic charm and flair, but you had to look past the exterior and overgrowth. In front of the house, there was a smaller driveway for parking in the shape of a horseshoe, with tiny pebble gravel, as if they meant it for a horse and buggy. There was a black antique metal horse's head pole used to tie up your horse by the front steps as a decorative piece. It seemed to draw you in to another era in time. There was a brick sidewalk which led to the steps on either side of the wrought-iron railing porch. The steps were a mirror image shape of the horseshoe driveway. There were white columns on either side of the porch that supported the overhang. This added a touch of style and elegance to the home.

The red brick exterior had Swedish Ivy that crept up the outer edges of the house, towards the roof and along the front steps. It gave the impression that the house was being suffocated. There were several huge, old oak trees in the front yard. Many overgrown and uprooted. I walked towards the back of the house and tried to avoid the tall weeds, but the tip end of my finger got pricked by the thistle.

"Ouch," I said as a tiny drop of blood oozed from my puncture site. I applied pressure to my finger to stop the bleeding. At that exact moment, I was hit with a flashback to my dream . . . running . . . prickly stems . . . blood droplets . . . stinging sensation. I gasped, not knowing what just happened.

As I continued to walk in the backyard, there were maple trees on top of the hillside, which provided a woodsy atmosphere along with patches of clay dirt on the ground. Another flashback came . . . a man . . . soldier . . . gray clothing . . . hole in the ground.

I panicked and said my mantra, "You can do this, Remi, just breathe." I stopped where I was standing and realized I had approached a rocky ledge where some trees had fallen and created an opening. While I was leaning over to take a quick glance, my foot slipped on a rock as it tumbled below, but I never heard it hit the bottom. This triggered a flashback from my dream again . . . edge of cliff . . . rocks . . . darkness . . . falling. My mouth fell open as I blurted out, "This property is the place in my dream." My heart started to race, and my breathing increased. I turned and ran back toward the front of the house.

The dreams I had through the years weren't always vivid. They seemed blurry and difficult to determine who or what was there. It still wasn't clear to me what the missing link might be in my dream or from the flashbacks I just encountered. I needed to share my flashbacks with Brock once we got settled and work on fitting the pieces of the puzzle together. In the meantime, I needed to gain my composure and get back to help set up the house. I would let Brock know about the cliff and the need for a safety fence to be put up in our backyard. This wasn't on the inspection list since it went past our property line, but I wouldn't want the kids or King to be tempted to wander over in that direction. My body shook by what I just experienced. When I reached the front of the house, I took a deep breath in and slowly released it several times. My breathing slowed down along with my heart rate. I was only back there ten minutes, but somehow it felt like forever.

The movers unloaded the furniture from the truck and our family entered through the front door of the home. Immediately, I was taken aback by a strong cigarette odor that hovered in the air. The hallway was dim, so I turned on the light and it flickered. King barked.

"King, it's okay. Calm down." Brock reached down to pat his head.

"Do you smell cigarette smoke?" I sniffed the air.

"No, I don't, but the house reeks of the chemicals the house cleaning crew used." Brock replied as he put his hand up to cover his mouth and nose. "Maybe the chemicals smell like cigarettes to you."

"It's freezing here in the hallway, which is odd since the air conditioner is off," I said, staring at the thermostat on the wall.

"It's ninety-five degrees outside. I'll set the thermostat to seventy-four and start cooling the rest of the house." Brock reached around me to adjust the temperature setting.

"What's up with the light?" I asked as King started to bark again. "It's okay, King. You're a good boy." I gave him a pat on the head.

"Remi, try not to worry so much. It was one item on the inspection list."

As I passed by the hallway, the light stayed on but no longer flickered, the cigarette odor faded, and the cool sensation in the hallway went away. King no longer barked.

"Is King always going to bark if the light flickers?"

Brock shrugged his shoulders and said, "He's a dog. Dogs bark at everything. Listen, I need to look through the rest of the house, so I can get the movers in here to unload our furniture. I'll unload the van after that."

"Sure thing," I said, as Brock hurriedly went on to another part of the house.

Dex, Londyn, and Nox ran upstairs, and each one found their own room. "This room is mine." Dex picked the blue one, which was the largest of the four rooms in the house's front side.

"I want this room." Londyn claimed the yellow room across from Dex.

"I guess I'm stuck with this room," said Nox with an air of disgust at the purple color on the walls.

I followed behind and walked Max up the steps for him to see his room, which was across the hall from Nox.

"This is my room." Max chimed in with a huge grin. "Where's King's room?"

"Don't worry about King. He can sleep in any room he wants," I said, hugging Max.

As I looked around at Max's room, I noticed wallpaper on one side of the room with little children playing on a farm with goats, sheep, and chickens and the other walls painted beige. I guess the previous owner had a child and never changed the room after he or she grew up.

King stayed close beside me while we checked out the upstairs. He had always been like a fifth child to me and thought he was human. We got him as a puppy when Dex was five. His jet black hair was soft as silk, and he had a white patch on his left ear. It was a birthmark he shared with his mother. King always acted like a child. He would jump in a chair at the kitchen table as he waited to be served. The kids got a kick out of that and would laugh.

"Hey, Mom, I put a bib on King. Now he needs some silverware and a plate," Dex said, laughing along with the other kids. He was an excellent guard dog for the family, too. King represented his name well in our household. I don't know what I would do without him.

A quick glance at both upstairs bathrooms revealed a need for cosmetic updates. They looked original to the house. The claw foot bathtubs were interesting with a hint of historic charm.

I turned on the upstairs hallway light to see if it had flicker issues, and it was the same results as downstairs. I felt that super cold sensation again, but now it was upstairs in the hall and it didn't feel like air conditioning. The cigarette smell was strong in this spot where I stood. King barked.

"What's wrong, King? It's okay. You're a good boy." I patted his head as a gesture of my appreciation. King acted unusual today whenever the lights flickered. I had never seen him react so defensively at an inanimate object.

Dex walked over and asked, "Mom, is it okay if we go outside and play in the backyard?"

"You can go outside, but stay in the front yard until we have a lawn crew come and clean up the thistles in back. Dex, you're in charge outside. Monitor Londyn and Nox."

"Don't worry, Mom, I will. Do you want me to take King outside, too?"

"That would be great."

Dex was a good big brother. I could count on him when I needed an extra pair of hands with his siblings. I think he enjoyed being in charge and liked to boss his brothers and sister around. It was not always effective, but I was grateful for his help. His siblings looked up to him since he was older.

As I turned to go back down the steps with Max, the hall light was still on. But I noticed the light flicker had stopped. The cigarette odor dissipated, the cool sensation subsided, and King no longer barked. Dex called King to follow after him, and they ran down the steps and out the front door together.

"Brock has got to check the wiring in this house even though the electrician couldn't pinpoint a problem," I murmured as I reached over to turn off the light switch.

Back downstairs on the main level were the living room, dining room, and kitchen in the traditional 1940s square room configuration. There was no open floor plan in this thirty-five hundred square foot home. Original oak floors were throughout the house and looked in good shape. There was a cleaning crew who buffed them before our arrival. Inside the house, it appeared the previous family had never worn shoes or had a pet running around. There were hardly any scuff marks. The floor boards in the kitchen were slightly wider than the rest of the house, which seemed odd that they weren't identical. The original owner must have replaced them at one time.

There was wallpaper on the walls in the kitchen, dining room, and bathrooms, which were now old, faded, and sparse. It would require some effort to remove what remained. I guess neither of us realized this house would be a challenge to fix up. We limited the home selections near the college and schools since we had to move and get settled before Brock started his new job.

A log fireplace was in the living room with bookshelves on either side. Walls were painted a pale pink with crown molding. Our master bedroom was located past the living room and down a hallway at the back of the house with white walls. It was secluded and great for privacy, but it was distant from the other part of the home, where the children would be sleeping. I hoped I could hear from Max if he woke up at night. We had used a baby monitor before when Max was an infant, but there was interference with our neighbors in the area using their baby monitor at the same time, and things came through like a walkie-talkie. Who knows what else the neighbors heard while that thing was on, so we donated it to a thrift store.

The basement was off from the kitchen. I went downstairs and took a quick look around. Part of it was finished and appeared to be neglected. There was an unfamiliar odor detected down there that was different from the rest of the house, and I wasn't sure where it came from. I noticed the concrete floor had unknown stains in places. The bathroom appeared to be an outhouse design, and the inside didn't look any better. Rotten wood shelves surrounded the work bench area. I touched one of the shelves and it fell down. On the far side near the wall, the heating and air unit made an odd clanging sound in the basement when Brock turned the air conditioning on earlier. The inspection showed if the clanging persisted, it may need to be updated. I put a note on my phone for Brock to have it rechecked. Towards the back door, there was a medium-sized room that was used for storage. The kids could use this room as a separate television room. After I looked around the house, it appeared we got more than we bargained for in fixing up this place. But we said we were up for the challenge, and we certainly got it with this home.

I had spoken with the secretary at Park Grove Elementary to arrange a new student transfer before we moved here. I made a call today so I could return the paperwork to the school as it would begin by the twenty-first of August. Throughout this moving process I said my mantra aloud, "You can do this, Remi, just breathe."

I headed to the kitchen with Max to unpack some boxes that had piled up on the floor. I noticed a piece of paper taped to the counter. It was from the house cleaning staff. The note said that while they cleaned, the lights flickered in the hallways and master bedroom. I guess they weren't aware this was on the inspection list. They also wrote there were continuous banging noises in the basement that sounded different from the occasional clanging from the air unit, even though no one was down there. They reported this to their supervisor, and the realtor told the house inspector.

Brock walked into the kitchen, and I put the note down to help him as he had unloaded the van with the last boxes that contained the food supply. I grabbed the note and showed it to him. Since the house inspector had already mentioned the lights, heat, and air conditioning unit on his list, Brock acknowledged the information on the note.

"I also wanted you to know I had flashbacks to my dream when I walked into the backyard earlier. This property was in my dream." There was more concern in my voice than expected.

"What makes you think that?" asked Brock with a puzzled look.

"When the thistle pricked my finger, and it bled, I immediately went back to my dream running through a field of prickly weeds scratching me and bleeding. When I looked at the hillside, the trees and barren spots seemed familiar and I remembered the soldier and grave. As I kept walking, I noticed a few trees along the back edge had fallen, and past that area was a rocky ledge. My mind took me straight to my dream of a rocky cliff edge and falling."

"That's odd. Have you had any flashbacks while inside the house?"

"No, only in the backyard. Do you think that's why we picked this house because it relates to my dream?"

"I'm not sure. Let's get settled, and if you have any more flashbacks, let me know right away, okay?"

"Okay, I will."

"And thanks for letting me know about the dangerous edge. It was on the inspection list as a concern, but it's not part of our property line. I'll get a fencing company to put up a fence along our backyard when the mowing crew removes the weeds."

Brock gave me a bear hug and a kiss to reassure me things would be fine as he headed outside to continue unloading items. I felt better sharing my flashbacks with Brock. He was a good listener.

I started working on emptying the boxes. The movers had brought in the kitchen table and chairs, and Max climbed up in his seat to eat his snack. "Okay, Max, time for mommy to get to work," I said, reaching for the shelf liner paper in the box. When I opened the first set of cabinets, the cleaning crew had already wiped down the shelves, which was a pleasant surprise. I started with the bottom shelf, unrolled the liner, and placed it inside. The white wooden cabinets looked deep and dark. I stocked the boxed and canned food items first.

When I got to the last top shelf, the liner hit something in the cupboard. I grabbed a two-step ladder, looked inside, and found an old metal bread box. It was beige with a faded yellow flower design beneath the red lid and rust showed its age. Inside was a dull-looking, round tin drinking cup with a bowed handle. On the bottom were the faded initials JA.

What was a tin cup doing inside a breadbox? Whoever put this up here didn't want anyone to find it. I thought.

The tin cup reminded me of being at Grandma Leona's. Her brother, Charles, had a similar tin cup from his service in the military. When he died, Grandma Leona kept his cup by her sink. I thought the tin cup I found might belong to the original homeowner, and he left it behind when he moved or died. I wasn't sure of the history of this house. The original owner must have served in the armed forces, too. I placed the tin cup by our kitchen sink as a reminder of my great Uncle Charles military service and for JA, whoever that might be.

"Now it feels like home, as if we were at Grandma Leona's place," I said proudly, displaying the treasured possession.

Throughout the years, age caused neglect to this beautiful old home. There was little information on the original home owners when Raheem set up the contract on the house. An attorney in Cedarville, along with a local real estate company, had taken over the sale of the house since there was no family to pass it to upon the owner's death. It had been on the market for twenty years. That was a long time for a house to be on the market. Maybe we should have asked more questions about the house before we bought it. But we had a time limit to move and get settled before school would start. Brock had visited the property and felt good about our decision.

This house was in a farming neighborhood and sold for less than the comparable value of the other homes on the same street. We purchased it at a bargain price which freed up funds to make the improvements. Every room needed a fresh coat of paint, the bathrooms and kitchen required updates, and the basement needed an overhaul. Brock was quite the handyman and planned to get started right away. I would pitch in and help in between managing the household.

I took a deep breath in and let it out slowly, saying my mantra, "You can do this, Remi, just breathe." At that moment, Brock walked in. I looked at him and said, "We have our work cut out for us."

"It'll take some time, but this house will have character once we breathe new life back into it," replied Brock, as he stepped closer, reaching out his arms to give me a much needed hug. My head fit snugly under his chin like a missing piece to a puzzle.

"I'm going to hold you to that," I said, inhaling the soothing smell of his spice cologne.

After we finished in the kitchen, the kids, King, and I headed upstairs. I pulled the clean sheets out of the bag on the floor. I wanted to set up the children's beds in each of their rooms. No matter how the rest of the house looked, everyone would sleep well tonight, after our long, grueling moving day. Each of the children would put away their own toys in their room and clothes in their dresser.

I would help Max with his room. His crib converted to a child size bed that he transitioned to before our move. His dresser and rocking chair completed the space.

When the children finished, they headed back outside to play and would monitor Max. King followed right behind them.

"Kids, stay in the front yard," I said.

I headed downstairs to the master bedroom and planned to unpack some boxes and make the bed. On the way, I smelled a stale cigarette odor, which was more prominent here than in the hallways. I felt a cool sensation as I passed by the living room and entered our bedroom. The hair on my arms and back of my neck stood up. The light on the ceiling in our bedroom flickered, and I heard a creak sound in the wooden floorboards of the living room as heavy footsteps followed behind me.

"Brock, is that you?" I spun around. No one was there. I walked back into the living room towards the front window and glanced out. All the movers finished unloading the truck and pulled out of the driveway. Brock was outside and unloaded more boxes from his car. I wondered where the kids went.

I headed back to our bedroom and looked out the rear window. The children and King ran and chased each other in the backyard.

"I thought I told them not to go back there." I muttered under my breath as I raised the window and yelled, "Kids, get in the front yard before you get scratched up from the weeds!"

They looked up with their mouths opened and their eyes widened as I had caught them playing where they had been told not to go. This was an expression I had seen them do many times before when they knew they were in trouble. The kids looked at each other and laughed as they said the word 'sorry' multiple times and ran towards the front yard with King right behind them.

I thought about the footstep sounds in the living room. If everyone was outside when it happened, whose footsteps were they? When Brock came to see the house before we moved in, he mentioned he heard footsteps upstairs. The air unit had recently been turned on by the inspector, so there wasn't any concern. The floorboards simply reacted to the coolness after the house sat empty for such a long time. The kids hadn't mentioned hearing or seeing anything strange. It was too late to back out of the house agreement now that we signed the contract. I thought my mind had played a trick on me, which made me feel uneasy about the move to this house. It was seventy-nine years old. Who knew what that sound might have been.

Maybe it was just my imagination. But something in the back of my mind told me not to let my guard down. Could this house have a haunted past?

CHAPTER THREE

I t was mid-afternoon on a gorgeous October day. The leaves had turned beautiful shades of red, orange, and yellow on the trees. We headed into the third month of living in our house.

Life had been good most of the time. The cigarette odor, light flicker, and cool sensation were still in the house along with a couple of other odd, unexplained experiences. One day, as I went in and out of the kitchen area, I noticed the tin cup had moved from the right side of the sink to the left, directly under the cabinet where I had originally found it. It was as if the tin cup wanted to go back inside. I asked Brock and the kids if they had touched the tin cup or if they had played a trick on me. They denied any involvement. How would a tin cup move all by itself?

Today was Brock's regular mowing day. He had finished around the front yard and started on the back. As he mowed, he saw something out of the corner of his eye. When he looked up towards the house, he thought there was someone at the window In Max's room, which was odd since the entire family was outside in the backyard. Brock suspected it was a shadow from a tree that appeared on the glass window. I wasn't sure about that since the trees were too far back on the hillside to leave a reflection. There was something creepy about this house and I wasn't certain it would be our permanent place to live. While the kids stayed outside in the yard, Brock and I went inside the house and upstairs to Max's room and found no one there. We checked the rest of the rooms in the house from top to bottom, but there was no one to be found.

"What do you think was in the window?" I questioned as Brock checked to make sure Max's window locked.

"I have no clue. I remember Ayesha saying her husband thought he saw something on the front window the day he trimmed the grass. I don't know if the two window scenes are similar or not. We'll need to keep a close eye out if any other strange things happen," Brock said with concern in his voice.

When Brock went back outside to continue mowing the lawn, I stayed in the house to see if whoever or whatever was out there would rear its ugly self again. I went to Dex's room and got his baseball bat, just in case I needed it for protection. I took a deep breath in and slowly let it out and said my mantra aloud, "You can do this, Remi, just breathe." But no one showed up.

During the weekdays, Brock's work at the college was going well, and he felt good about the decision he made with his new job. The children had adjusted to their new school and connected with friends. On the weekends, Brock worked diligently on his fix-it-list for the house. We hadn't noticed anymore dark shady figures in the windows from outside or seen any in the house after that one incident.

The past few months had been busy with house updates. The kids were excited about the rec room in the basement that was completed. It would be a great hangout away from the parents to binge watch television and play games.

On the days when Brock was at work and the kids were at school, Max and I had our own daily routine around the house. King had adjusted to the new home but stayed by my side as he guarded me while the kids were at school. It was unusual for King to be this clingy.

One of my projects in the house was wallpaper removal and painting. I rented a wallpaper steamer and had a three-prong attachment to use in the outlet. The steamer would make it easier to scrape off the little pieces of wallpaper that were left on the walls. In our master bathroom, I received a minor shock when I plugged the steamer into the outlet. As I flipped the switch to turn on the machine, it immediately turned off without me touching it. The lights in the bathroom flickered, stale cigarette smoke lingered around, and I felt a cool sensation in the small space. Without warning, the steamer machine turned back on by itself. I wasn't sure what happened with the outlet, the device, or the bathroom atmosphere.

The steam rental company would provide another unit. I made a note for Brock about the light flicker and the outlet adapter shock. It was odd since I never had that problem when I used the same outlet to plug in my hair dryer.

Today I would remove the wallpaper the old-fashioned way with soapy water in a spray bottle and a scraper. When I completed the task, the light stopped its flicker, the cigarette smoke went away, and the cool sensation left the room. As I glanced around, I noticed a small smudge was on the left upper corner of the bathroom mirror that wasn't there earlier. The wallpaper removal product must have left a splatter mark on it. I used a tissue to wipe it off, which didn't work. I tried using plain water and soapy water to clean the mirror. No matter how hard I tried, the smudge wouldn't go away. I left it alone since the mirror was original to the house and I didn't want to make it worse.

Over the next few days, Brock followed up on the flicker with the lights and outlets. He had a background in electrical technology and learned this trade as a kid working alongside his father, who was a licensed electrician. Brock noticed a few light bulbs needed to be changed, but the wiring was actually in good condition and didn't require any replacement. The electrician had confirmed this on the home inspection, too. The old electrical outlets needed an update to make sure they were up to code. Some of the lighting fixtures in the ceiling would need replacement. Hopefully, these changes would resolve the problem.

The most troubling aspect for me was the cigarette odor and coolness in the air that would come and go throughout the house. It was more noticeable and stronger in the master bedroom in the evenings while Brock and I were watching television. It seemed as if I was the only one affected by it and didn't understand the reason. There was no mention of it by either Brock or the kids, so I tried not to think about it.

In the back of my mind, I always had an odd feeling that someone watched us closely. Whoever had eyes on us followed every move we made and every update completed. I could sense that whatever was in the house wasn't happy with the changes. Our family had invaded its living space. Could that shadowy figure Brock thought he saw in the rear window and the dark area on the front window that Ayesha's husband had seen be a spirit dwelling in our house? Was this the reason behind the unexplained occurrences?

No matter what strange things transpired, Brock enjoyed living here. He was in his element as he spent time outdoors, worked in the yard, and fixed things. The kids loved the big backyard as they ran free, played games, and watched King chase after them. I noticed King hadn't been as clingy around me as he was when we first moved in. He appeared to be more comfortable as he got into his own daily routine. But each night King chose a different bedroom in the house to sleep while he kept guard over our family. He still barked whenever the lights flickered.

As I walked through the house one day, I felt a strange sensation that someone had breathed down the back of my neck. When I turned around, no one was there. That feeling occurred throughout our entire home, as if I was being followed. I never heard Brock or the kids complain about this sensation. If my assumption was correct, whoever or whatever this thing was that hung out in our home would not be quiet for much longer. I believed our family had awakened some kind of spirit in this house that had been dormant for the past twenty years. What would happen to our family whenever this entity finally revealed itself to us?

Today the kids were at school, Brock was at work, and Max was lying down for a nap. Out of the four kids, Max was the most restless with sleeping. The slightest noise at night would startle him. Even now, Max would still wake up and want something to drink or use the bathroom. He was a light sleeper like me.

Max called out for me after his nap. King and I got him and walked downstairs to the kitchen where he sat at the table and munched on a snack, along with a juice box drink.

"Can I play ball?" mumbled Max with a mouthful of crackers.

"Max, swallow your food. You want to play whiffle ball outside?" I asked as Max polished off the last cracker.

"Yes," said Max, shaking his head in agreement.

"Okay, let's go back upstairs and get your things."

After his snack, we gathered everything and went into the backyard to play. King followed behind and rested in the yard.

"I'm thirsty," Max announced after playing one round of ball.

"Okay, go inside and get some water. The kitchen door is open." I instructed, and watched Max head inside.

The refrigerator's ice and water dispensers were on one side of the door for Max to reach them. But I realized Max was too small to get the cups out of the cabinet, and I wouldn't want him climbing on the counters. As I approached the bottom of the first porch step to go inside and help him, Max was already out the back door and stood on the deck. He had two plastic tumbler cups of ice water filled to the brim. He spilled the water as he walked towards me. How did he open the door with his hands so full?

"Here, Mommy." Max handed one of the drink cups to me.

"Max, how did you reach the cups in the cabinet?" I asked, with a puzzled look.

"Jack helped me." Max explained.

I looked at Max in disbelief and repeated what he said. "Jack helped you?"

"Yeah, Jack."

"Who's Jack?"

"He's my friend." Max stood there as he drank his water, which started to leak from his mouth onto his shirt.

I took Max by the hand and quickly headed back into the house. I searched every square inch of our home from top to bottom. The front door and basement doors were locked. All of the windows were locked, too. The only door open was the back kitchen door. Max and I were in the yard with a full view of the back porch and no one entered or exited. I don't know who Jack was or how he got into the house, but Max saw him.

"Max, where did you see Jack?"

"Over there," said Max as he pointed to the kitchen sink counter where the tin cup sat.

"What did Jack look like?"

"He was big." Max put both hands straight up and wide and tilted his head back towards the ceiling.

"Was Jack tall?"

"Yeah, he's tall."

"What did Jack do?"

"He got me cups. I got some water."

"How did you get the door open while carrying the cups?"

"Jack did it."

"Where did Jack go after he helped you?"

"He had work. He left."

"Did you see Jack walk out the door?"

"No, he stayed. He left that way." Max pointed towards the front hallway.

I kept Max inside the house in case his friend Jack showed up again. I wanted to see for myself whoever or whatever Jack might be. We went upstairs to Dex's room, and I got his baseball bat and took it downstairs to keep by my side. I called for King to come back in the house. The three of us sat at the kitchen table as I turned on the wall mounted TV for Max to watch a show while I anxiously waited to see if Jack would return. But no one showed up.

Later that evening, when Brock had come home from work, I told him about Max's remark of someone named Jack who helped him with his water. Brock wasn't sure what to make of the situation. Our Christian upbringing didn't leave room for believing in ghosts that haunted a dwelling after their death. Your soul went to heaven or hell. There was no lingering around on earth. A person's choice was already made when he or she died. Brock was more skeptical about spirit entities than me. I had a sense of connection with the afterlife since childhood. Now, our discussion was about a spirit entity in our home that our child actually met in a face-to-face encounter.

Our family hadn't attended church as often as we should have back in Millburg. Life got in the way with Brock's work and the kid's activities, so we put our church on the back burner. Now, with a possible spirit in the house, this would be an excellent opportunity to find a church home right here in Cedarville and rethink about attending again. If our family could find a local church, we could keep our faith strong with our focus on God and His word. Maybe this would help us get rid of Jack's spirit from our home. Our family shouldn't have to live in fear inside the house we just bought and moved into. I wouldn't allow whoever Jack was to control us. This wasn't his house anymore.

Brock walked into the bedroom as I stood by the dresser and asked, "You know, Max was serious when he answered my questions about Jack. How do you know if our son saw a figment of his imagination or something else not of this world?"

Brock shrugged his shoulders and said, "Max is at that age where make-believe friends seem real. I'm sure he's already forgotten about it."

"An imaginary friend wouldn't have helped Max get glasses out of the cabinet. The dishwasher was empty, and no dishes were in the dish drain, counter, or table. How do you explain that?" I asked, pacing back and forth.

"I don't have an answer for that. I know we had a shadowy figure show up in the window one day, but that doesn't mean it was a spirit or 'Jack.' Just try to relax, Remi," said Brock, as he reached out his arms and pulled me close for a big hug. I always melted in his arms when he hugged me. After that, anything else that was on my mind didn't matter.

When Brock and I went to bed that night, I replayed Max's remark about Jack in my mind. Had this spirit actually helped him with the cups in the cabinet? How could he see a dead man? I wanted to believe he saw this entity, but kids were impressionable at his age. Something he saw on television or heard from his siblings probably influenced him. It didn't even matter to him that this stranger was in our house. Max wasn't afraid of Jack. Could he have made up this name? Was it Jack's breath I felt on the back of my neck? Were his eyes the ones that watched us all this time in the house? Call it women's intuition or a hunch; I always knew we weren't alone and never would be as long as we lived in this house. What would be Jack's next move?

CHAPTER FOUR

T he one thing I had begun to fear since we moved into our home had come true. As much as I tried to push it aside, when I stepped foot onto this property and entered the inside of this house, the sense that there was a spirit entity watching us had become reality. Now, I knew his name . . . JACK. Our son, Max, saw Jack. How was that even possible?

I would protect our family from this spirit entity living in our home, but how? It was no longer his house, but our house. What does Jack want? Why would his spirit not leave our home? If he wanted to frighten me, it worked. It certainly helped explain the light flicker, the cigarette smoke, and the cool sensation that hovered in the room. It also explained how I heard heavy footstep sounds behind me in the living room and felt someone's breath on the back of my neck. Yet no one was there. Was he the reason behind the electrical outlets causing a shock to me? When the tin cup moved to a different place in the kitchen, was he responsible?

When Jack helped Max with the water, I wasn't clear what his intentions might be. Why would he disclose himself only to Max? Whatever reason Jack may have had, I would not subject the family to anything else he might try to do. But how do you stop something you can't see?

Brock and I sat at the kitchen table and drank our coffee when I asked, "Do you think Jack's spirit might harm our family? I'm worried about the kids."

"Right now, Jack's spirit only revealed himself to Max one time. And yes, that's a little unsettling. I know you've mentioned before the cigarette smell, the cool sensation, and the feeling of someone breathing down the back of your neck. The kids and I haven't had that experience. Maybe with your connection to the afterlife, your senses are more in touch with spirit encounters. I understand your concern. I wish I had an answer to your question. All we can do is take things one day at a time and hope that this spirit doesn't come back again. We need to live our lives the way we always do. This is a wonderful house for our family." Brock validated Remi's concerns as he reached out and gave her a hug.

"I hope you're right." I wondered what might happen next.

On a sunny weekend afternoon in November, I approached Brock as he read the paper in the living room.

"Honey," I asked, "could you watch the children for a couple of hours? I need some me time and I thought I might go to Mumford to look around at the shops."

"Sure, I'll work on some projects around the house on my list. The kids will be fine. Enjoy your alone time."

I gave Brock a kiss and headed out the door. What I didn't tell Brock was I had an appointment thirty minutes away in downtown Mumford with a psychic medium named Madame Tallulah. I found Madame Tallulah during an internet search, and she came highly recommended.

I wasn't one who usually believed in the work a medium performed, but I felt the need to talk to someone else about our spirit intrusion, and this seemed like a good option.

Mumford was a smaller town than Cedarville. The shops along West Avenue downtown were locally owned businesses inside of older renovated buildings. Decorative flower pots hung from the street lamp posts, which added a punch of color to the downtown area. There were pansies planted inside the pots in shades of yellow and purple, with a hint of additional winter greenery sprinkled in the mix.

Madame Tallulah's business was in an old white paneled storefront building on the corner of West Avenue and Court Street. I parked the van and hesitantly walked up to the red front door. I wasn't sure what to expect from this meeting and found myself really nervous. The door had cracked paint and a rusty gargoyle knocker. That's interesting, I mused. Upon my knocking, an elderly woman greeted me. I assumed this to be Madame Tallulah.

I wasn't sure what to expect when I met Madame Tallulah. She looked like your average elderly grandmother, with a hint of vintage finesse. She had sharp facial features with a square jaw, glassy blue eyes, and a big, wide smile with stained yellow teeth from age and possibly lots of coffee. She also had a slight, tiny gap between her two front teeth. Madame Tallulah had a gypsy style about her as she adorned herself in a multi-colored dress, faded gold link chains around her neck, and big shiny gold loop earrings. Her multiple tarnished silver bracelets clanged with each movement of her hands. She seemed fidgety and nervous, as if she had too much caffeine in her system. Her dark scarf and gold headband covered part of her curly gray hair that flowed down past her shoulders. Madame Tallulah's posture hunched over slightly. It resulted from leaning over her table doing psychic readings for who knows how many years.

"Come, come my child. Enter my abode," said Madame Tallulah, as she held out her right hand and gestured me to come inside.

I couldn't tell if her accent was real or fake, but it sounded nasally and high pitched like a wicked old witch from a television show. Madame Tallulah led me through the front entryway, which was brightly lit with naked walls and no furniture. We headed towards the back through eggplant colored velveteen curtains into a room with a pink fluorescent light high in the center of the ceiling. The walls were a dark color, and from high on the wall hung mystical pictures of forests, mushrooms, and psychedelic abstract designs in rainbow colors. A black light caused the pictures to appear in a 3-D image, which jumped off the wall right at me. It felt as if I had stepped back in time to the seventies. There was incense that burned in the back corner of the room, which had the aroma of rosemary and sandalwood. Now, all we needed was a strobe light and some head banging music to complete the mood.

"I'll take the money up front before we begin. Fifty dollars for ten minutes," said Madame Tallulah, as she stood there with her right arm extended and her palm open to receive the money.

"Oh, yes." I fumbled in my purse for the cash. My eyes had a hard time focusing without sufficient light.

"I thought your website said it was fifty dollars for one hour, not ten minutes." I paid Madame Tallulah, and she immediately grabbed the cash with her long, slender fingers and even longer fingernails. They looked like sharp knives with dark, chipped nail polish.

"No, it's ten minutes. I didn't make that website. I'm too old to learn computers. You've already paid, and there are no refunds. Do you wish to continue?" asked Madame Tallulah.

"Well, yes, I want to get my money's worth."

"Then, let us begin."

Madame Tallulah gestured me to follow her. "Here, my dear. Have a seat," she said as she pulled out a chair for me to sit down.

Madame Tallulah had a circular table in the center of the room with a black tablecloth that went to the floor and in the middle was a crystal ball. She had two chairs with faded velvet seats and a dark ornate backing that had the shape of blackbirds carved into the wood. Madame Tallulah fixated her eyes on the crystal ball as her hands hovered over it and said, "Oh, yes, yes, I see."

I felt like I had seen this same scenario played out before in a movie. I wondered if there was a hidden camera, as I scoured every inch of the room from floor to ceiling. I didn't see any flashing red light since the lighting was too bad to see clearly. At any minute, I expected someone to jump out from behind the velveteen curtain and yell 'Surprise!'

"You're not from around here, are you?" inquired Madame Tallulah, with her elbows on the table as she tapped her bony fingers together.

"No, I live in Cedarville," I answered.

"My child, you're here about a spirit haunting your home?" asked Madame Tallulah as she hovered closely over the crystal ball.

"Yes, that's correct." I noticed smoke filled the inside of the crystal ball as if by magic. What did she have under the table to make that happen?

"Aw, I see the spirit's name has the letter 'J' in it?"

"Yes, that's right."

"I can see that the spirit's name is Jack. Is that correct?"

"Why yes, how did you know?"

"I know all things," said Madame Tallulah with a boast of confidence. "I see darkness over your house. It's haunted. I sense fear from you because of this spirit."

"Yes, the spirit is doing things in the house to scare our family. Jack is nice to our three-year-old son who actually saw him in our kitchen. Do you know how that could happen?"

"Your child is in an early stage of his life and has an open mind not crowded by lies, deceit, and evil. He may see a spirit now, but as he grows older, the ability to see the spirit will leave; if he chooses to no longer believe."

"What should I do about the spirit? I want him out of our house."

"Wait, I see another spirit. This is not Jack. I don't know this spirit. He's not in the house. He's outside the house surrounded by other spirits."

"I had a dream about a soldier when I was a child. I think I'm having the same dream as an adult, but the image keeps fading and getting darker. Is the soldier from my dream the spirit?"

"My child, I can see that your house is in a spirit battle. It must stop before evil wins."

"Is Jack the evil one or the other spirit?"

"That's for you to decide. You must have your house cleansed to rid all of the spirits away. Go and seek professional help as soon as possible."

"But, who do I contact? What does a house cleanse entail?" The smoke inside the crystal ball started to fade. Did Madame Tallulah use a control device in her hand or was it hidden under the table?

"Your ten minutes is up. The crystal ball can no longer see into your present or future. More questions requires more money."

"Oh, I see. Well, uh, thank you, Madame Tallulah. That's all the money I have. Are you sure that was ten minutes? It feels like we just got started." Was her crystal ball a timer? After ten minutes the smoke would disappear and the client would need to go home? Pretty clever.

"Your time started when you entered through the front door. You know where to exit. Good day," said Madame Tallulah, as she flicked her wrist and pointed for me to head through the velveteen curtains that led to the front door. Madame Tallulah got up from her chair and walked through another door in the back. I heard a television and other people talking. The sweet smell of cigar smoke and a pungent aroma of alcohol filled the air. Someone had soundproofed the room for me not to have heard anything.

I left the psychic medium wondering how she knew so much about our home and spirit invasion. Had she talked with someone before I came or had she known the history of my house all these past twenty years while it was vacant? What had she meant by more spirits outside the home? Would that have anything to do with my dream about the soldier? She never really answered my question. Madame Tallulah was a mystery herself. Brock wouldn't be happy knowing I spent fifty dollars on a psychic medium. But desperate times call for desperate measures. This was one of them.

After I left Madame Tallulah's, I browsed through some of the local shops and picked up a few treats for the kids. I still had fifty minutes left on the parking meter, and I had to prove I attempted to shop.

When I arrived back at the house, all four children were in the basement rec room as they laughed and played. "Hey kids, I'm back. I brought each of you some treats to share. Do any of you need anything else?" I asked, as Nox threw a soft sponge ball, which veered in my direction and bounced off my head.

"Sorry about that, Mom. I was throwing it to Londyn," Nox answered, covering his mouth to hold back a giggle.

"I'm glad they made the ball out of sponge," I quipped.

"Max is playing trucks with Dex," Londyn replied, trying to turn her head away as she laughed.

"We have a handle on things, Mom. Thanks for the treats," said Dex.

"This is a big truck," Max announced as he held it up proudly.

"Please don't throw that at me," I joked.

The kids seemed content. I was glad they were self-sufficient. Brock was outside as he mowed the lawn on his riding mower with his headphones on to drown out the noise while he protected his one good ear. King rested quietly in the backyard while he soaked up the fall sunshine. I stood on the back porch and waved to Brock to get his attention that I was back home, and he acknowledged me with a wave of his hand.

Since everyone had been doing their own thing, I worked on some routine house chores. Maybe this could be part of my cleansing that Madame Tallulah talked about. I headed downstairs to the basement for the cleaning supplies and took them upstairs to the master bedroom. I cranked the stereo up to keep me motivated while I cleaned.

In the bathroom, I headed to the shower stall, took out the hand-held sprayer, and turned on the water. I got down on my hands and knees while I sprayed with one hand and scrubbed with the other. The songs blared from the stereo speaker as I sang along to the music. Steam built up which fogged the bathroom. I forgot to turn on the ceiling fan. As I pushed up from my kneeling position, I felt a hand slap on my backside, which stung.

"What was that? Brock, is that you?" I asked aloud, as I dropped the hand sprayer, shocked by what occurred.

I looked behind me, and no one was there. I left the bathroom, checked the bedroom, and found it empty. When I called out to the kids and Brock, no one responded. Looking out the back bedroom window, Brock was still mowing. At a brisk pace, I headed downstairs to the basement. The kids had settled down and sat quietly while they watched a television show.

"Did anyone come upstairs in the bathroom to see me just now?" I asked, puzzled.

"No," replied the children in unison.

I went back to the master bedroom, perplexed by what I had felt earlier. In the bathroom, the water from the hand sprayer spewed everywhere. The steam fogged up the mirror, and there was a name written on it in big capital letters . . . TORI. The moisture caused the name to run at the bottom of each letter as if blood oozed from it.

I gasped and asked aloud, "What the . . . who wrote this? Who's Tori?"

I left the bathroom, grabbed my phone off the dresser, and took a photo of the words written on the mirror. This was proof that someone was definitely in the house. I turned off the shower water and stopped cleaning. No one had been in this room to write this name.

"Did you write this, Jack? Are you trying to scare me? My name is not Tori. Go away and leave us alone!" I said aloud in anger, looking around, expecting Jack to show his face.

At that moment, Brock finished mowing the lawn. He popped his head through the back kitchen door and yelled, which startled me. "Remi, come outside! You've got to see this." I left the bedroom and headed to the kitchen. Brock stood on the back porch.

"Come out here and see what King found in the backyard."

I went outside, down the back steps. King sat there proudly as he guarded a rusty grenade he had dug up in the dirt outside the shed door.

"What on earth is that thing? Is it real?" I asked, confused by what I saw.

"It looks like an old hand grenade. I'm going to take a photo and share it with the college librarian, Linda Eastin. When I go to the college on Monday, I want to see if Linda can look up the details on the grenade type and the specific war era. In the meantime, I need to call the local authorities and have it inspected just to be on the safe side and off our property."

Brock pulled out his phone and contacted the Cedarville Police Department. They had an officer downtown that would be at our house in the next twenty minutes to inspect the grenade. In the meantime, Brock would wait on mowing the rest of the lawn until the officer arrived.

A police cruiser pulled up in our driveway. Brock went out to greet the uniformed officer, Sergeant Hernandez, and escorted him to the back of our house as he handed him the grenade.

"Ay, dios mio. Where did you find this grenade?" asked Sergeant Hernandez, while holding the object delicately in his hands.

"Our dog dug it up right here in the backyard," explained Brock as he pointed to the hole King left in the yard.

"It's quite unusual for a grenade to be in the backyard of a residential area. I wonder how it ended up here, of all places. I don't believe this is an active grenade, but I'll take it back to the station and have someone look at it."

"Thank you. We appreciate you arrived here so quickly. Please keep us posted on what you learn," Brock said.

As Sergeant Hernandez left, Brock and I looked at each other, not knowing what to make of the situation. If there was a grenade in our yard, what other items might be buried along with it? What made King go to that specific spot in the yard and start digging, anyway? Something had to attract him to that site. The only thing I could think of at the moment was Jack.

"Who are you, Jack? What do you want from us?" I yelled with my fists clenched tight.

At that moment, I realized I had not shown Brock my photo. I pulled my phone from my pants pocket and pulled up the picture I had taken of the name TORI on the bathroom mirror.

"Brock, look at this photo. It appeared on the mirror in our bathroom while I was cleaning. Who or what is Tori?" I asked.

"Whoa, that's strange. I have no clue what the name Tori means. Are you sure the kids didn't write something on the mirror last night and it showed up today when the steam got on it?"

"No, the children haven't been back in our room. They've been using the basement or the upstairs bathroom. If they did do it, it still doesn't explain who Tori could be."

"Maybe it's a character from one show they watch or a video game they play. Maybe Dex has a girlfriend at school by that name." Brock gave a wink and a smile.

"Stop joking, Brock. I'm serious. If one of our children did do this, what would be the purpose of writing that name on our bathroom mirror?"

"It beats me. Are you thinking this is something Jack might have done to scare us? Is that why you were yelling his name earlier?"

"I don't know what to think. But it worries me. I won't lie about that."

Brock reached out his arms and gave me a hug for reassurance, and said, "Let me finish in the yard. Why don't you go inside and see what the kids have to say about the name."

I headed back inside the house and took King along with me. The children remained in the rec room and were ready to head outside to play. Before going out, I asked Dex, Londyn, and Nox if either of them had been in our bathroom recently.

"No," they said in unison.

"Wait, I used the bathroom one time when the other ones were full," said Dex.

"When was that?" I asked.

"I don't know. It may have been today or yesterday."

"Did you write anything on the mirror while you were in there?"

"No, Mom. Why would I do that? Why are you asking me that question?"

"I was just wondering. Okay, go on outside and play while there's still daylight."

"Parents are so weird," remarked Dex under his breath.

The children left the rec room and ran out the basement door to go play in the backyard. There had to be a reason the name Tori was on our bathroom mirror and why someone named Jack was in our house. I needed more information on who lived here before our family occupied this home. The deed to the house with the original owner's name was what I needed. Somehow we never received a copy on closing. A trip downtown to the courthouse might lead me to some answers. It was Saturday, and I could do nothing until Monday. I would need to wait.

CHAPTER FIVE

I t was an overcast Monday in November. Brock and I had waited patiently for Sergeant Hernandez to call us about the hand grenade King found in our yard. When we received the call, he confirmed the hand grenade was not active. Brock and I breathed a sigh of relief. Brock informed Sergeant Hernandez he found no other military items in the hole where King had dug earlier.

"By the way, I also wanted to share with you that the hand grenade was from the Civil War Era. I'm not sure why it would have been on your property. There have been rumors in the past of a possible cemetery on the premises. But I found no paperwork to confirm that information," explained Sergeant Hernandez.

That was interesting news we weren't expecting. We thanked Sergeant Hernandez for everything he had done.

I looked over at Brock and asked quizzically, "The Civil War Era? A cemetery? My dream has a soldier in it wearing gray clothing. Do you think the grenade and the soldier have a connection?"

"It almost seems that way, doesn't it? Maybe this will help you find the answers you've been waiting for to fill the void in your dreams." Brock's voice held an air of excitement.

"We shall see." I didn't want to jump to conclusions yet.

This past weekend I wasn't only concerned about the grenade, but I was curious about finding more information on who Jack could be. Why had he invaded our home? What was the meaning behind the name Tori? Why was there a grenade buried in our backyard and who had it really belonged to? Was any of this connected? I was about to find out.

I got the van ready and took Max along. We headed to the Emery County Courthouse outside of Cedarville for help in obtaining the name of the original owner of our property. There had to be a reason for Jack's spirit living in our home. Had he died in the house? Was his body buried somewhere on the property? Was Tori the name of someone Jack wanted us to know about?

We pulled up to the courthouse on Campbell Street. It was an old two-story white brick building with gray slate steps and matching ramp which led up to the front door. There were glass windows on either side. I parked in the lot across the street and we headed into the building. A young college student manned the front desk. I informed him of my appointment with Ming Choo. He motioned me to have a seat to wait while he contacted her office.

Ming Choo, who was Clerk of the Circuit Court, came out of her office to the waiting area. She was a petite lady with coal black hair pulled back in a round bun. Her red silk dress had gold flower inlays on the front and back with a matching headband. She looked like an actress ready to attend a formal affair at a star-studded premiere show.

"Hello, I'm Ming Choo. You must be Mrs. Sterling."

"Hi, Ms. Choo. I have an appointment with you about the original deed to our home. We purchased the house on Westview

Lane. Here is a copy of our contract, a proof of our current ownership and my driver's license with our current address." I handed over the paper and my license to Ms. Choo. She looked them over and nodded her head in approval before handing them back to me.

"Yes, I believe I have what you need in our files. Please, follow me, Mrs. Sterling."

I pushed Max along in his stroller as I followed Ming Choo down a long corridor and into a separate room with a table and two chairs. Max was well-behaved as he ate his snack while I waited on Ming Choo to retrieve the deed. Cedarville was not up-to-date like Millburg which offered deeds to houses online for viewing. The only way I could see the deed was at the courthouse to review the copy.

Quickly, she presented me with the deed. She excused herself to go answer another question and told me she would be back in a few minutes. When she left, I stared closely at the deed in my hands. I saw the original homeowner's name that stood out as plain as day in big bold black letters JACK and his wife VICTORIA Aster.

"Oh my," I gasped under my breath as I saw both of their names together on the deed. I stared at the name Victoria and the name TORI jumped right off the page at me in a 3-D image effect. My heart skipped a beat, and my cheeks felt flushed.

As I looked over the deed, I remarked under my breath, "Max really saw Jack in the house. What happened to make that possible? And, Jack's wife was named Victoria or Tori for short. That must have been his nickname for her and the name that he wrote on the mirror in our bathroom. How could a spirit do that?

Jack's last name was Aster. His initials were JA. Was that his tin cup I found hidden in the kitchen cabinet? Why would he hide his own tin cup?"

Just then, Ming Choo's return to the room startled me. "Are you okay, Mrs. Sterling? You look like you've seen a ghost."

"No, I mean yes, thank you. I'm okay. Can you tell me how to find out who was the builder of the house and anything about the property?"

"Yes, you'll need to drive five blocks towards the downtown area to the Municipal Building. It will be at the corner of Market Square and Cape Avenue. Jace Stephen is the Building Commissioner, and he can help you."

"Could I have a copy of this deed for our records at home?"

"Why yes, I'll get that done and have it ready for you on your way out."

"Thank you, Ms. Choo, for your help."

As Max and I left the building and headed back to the van, I was in shock that the name Jack and Victoria were on the original deed. They were both real. Max actually saw Jack. I wondered what had happened to Jack and Victoria. How was his spirit in the house that we lived in and not Victoria's?

Max fell asleep on our short drive over to the Municipal Building. I parked the van on the street and carefully moved Max into the stroller and proceeded toward the entrance.

The Municipal Building was one level with orange brick, brown double-wide wooden doors, and clear glass windows. As I entered, a gentleman stood behind the front desk next to the Administrative Assistant and greeted me.

"Hi, I'm Jace Stephen. You must be Remi Sterling," he introduced himself, and reached out his hand to shake mine.

"Why yes, that's correct." I said, looking closely at his face. His steely blue eyes and square jaw looked familiar. Where had I seen those same facial features?

"Let's head down to my office where it'll be more comfortable for you and your son."

Jace escorted me down the hall as I pushed a sleeping Max along. He motioned me to sit in a chair across the desk from him. Jace informed me he had received a call from Ming Choo and handed me the original building permit file for our house.

Along with the permit, there were photographs of the property before and after the home was built. First, the contents of the photo, after they built the house, drew me right to it. There was a dark mist which hovered outside over the roof. There may have been a storm on the horizon. But I remembered the picture Ayesha had shown us when we chose the house. And on the day we moved in, there was a similar dark cloud. I doubted this was a coincidence. What could it mean? Next, I noticed that the land in the photo, before they built the house, looked familiar.

I gasped and mumbled under my breath, "It looks like my dream."

"I'm sorry. You said something about a dream," Jace repeated.

"Oh, nothing. I was just talking to myself. Careless habit," I said as I rolled my eyes and bit my lip to keep my mouth closed.

As I continued to look over the information, the home was built in 1940 by JV Contracting, Incorporated. Those were the first initials of Jack and his wife, Victoria. They owned the company and started it right after they married. Victoria managed the business end while Jack handled the construction part. Apparently, the company was successful and had made a great deal of money. They obviously made a talented team.

"So, you're the family that bought the Aster place. You know, people say it's haunted," said Jace.

"Haunted? What do you mean?" I probed, already aware of what he meant but wanted to hear his version.

Jace informed me of how his grandparents knew Jack and Victoria Aster. Victoria had gone to the same Catholic Church as his grandparents, and they talked about everything. Jace mentioned it was only Jack and Victoria that lived in their house. They could have no kids of their own. They only had each other and Victoria's multiple Siamese cats she had through the years.

"Victoria loved cats like children. They were inseparable," said Jace. "She had one cat at a time and it would follow her everywhere she went, even to their contracting job sites."

"You said the house is haunted. Could you tell me more? Also, do you know anything else about the original owner and the background of the house?"

"Certainly. I'll tell you the short version of the story."

Jace filled me in about the Aster property, which sat on four acres of land and handed down to Jack in a will by his father. People would say that there used to be an old cemetery on the property with military ties from the late 1800s, but there was no written document found to support it. No one had properly maintained the site. Tombstones or markers were decayed or stolen through the years and the cemetery forgotten. Plant and weed overgrowth, along with uprooted and downed trees, ruined whatever was once there on the property.

When Jack and his wife inherited the land, Jack had it bulldozed, and that's where they built their house. He was not a religious man and had told everyone he was an atheist. Any bodies buried there; the bulldozer had destroyed. Victoria wasn't aware of any cemetery on the property, or she would have stopped Jack. She was a religious person and would never deface a graveyard to build a house. Jack could be tough and mean in getting what he wanted.

After Jack and Victoria had died, kids at school would talk about old man Aster and his house that sat on top of the soldiers' graves. It became a dare about the feuding ghosts and who would be the first to go inside the house to hear them fight. One night, some kids took on the challenge and went into the vacated house. Once inside, they heard footsteps and a banging sound in the basement. In the master bedroom area, someone walked around and a popping noise was heard, like gunshots fired. This had to be the ghosts who feuded back and forth. Dead soldiers wanted to get out of the graveyard under the house, but Jack held them hostage with his gun. They ran out of the house as fast as their little legs would take them. Each kid went straight home and told their parents what they had heard.

Once the rumor spread that there was a ghost in the house, no one wanted to buy it. There were some prospective buyers who were skeptical about the rumor but decided later they wouldn't want to take a chance on living there.

"Jace, earlier you mentioned Jack was mean. Can you explain that further?"

"Well, my grandparents had told my parents that Jack was a hell-raiser back in the day. He always had a rifle and threatened to harm anybody that stepped foot onto his property. He was protective with his house and land."

"What made him act that way?"

"He was a changed man when he came back from war."

Jace said the army drafted Jack in 1941 and he served two years in WWII. While Jack carried out his duties, he got a head injury from an explosion. He came back home in 1943, got a purple heart for his bravery, and disabled the rest of his life.

"What about his wife, Victoria? Do you know if Jack had a nickname for her?"

"According to my grandparents, Tori was the name Jack used. No one else could call her by that name."

Jace was like an encyclopedia of information and kept on with the conversation. As the years had gone by, Victoria held onto the contracting company she and Jack owned until she turned sixty-five and retired. She had too much to do with keeping a constant eye on Jack. His mind had gotten worse as the years progressed.

"Jack threatened Victoria a few times. As a matter-of-fact, the kitchen caught on fire and the back of the house burned in 1998. The wood stove blew up when Jack accidentally threw gasoline into the fire on top of the wood, trying to make the fire get hotter. He wasn't aware of what he was doing."

"Oh, my. What happened to Jack and Victoria?"

"Well, unfortunately, Victoria and their latest cat died," Jace explained, as he continued sharing about the Asters. Victoria was seventy-nine years old when she died, and Sam, the last of their ten cats, was just three. Jack got burned and barely survived the fire. His mental condition deteriorated further when he learned Victoria had died. She was the love of his life. Nothing mattered except her. He would do anything to get her back. Jack's insurance company covered the repair costs to fix up the back of the home while he was in the rehabilitation hospital recuperating from his burns. They ruled the fire accidental because of Jack's mental status and the fact that Victoria was with him. Before Jack got out of the hospital, a judge ruled him incapacitated and the town's attorney became his legal guardian over his medical and financial well-being. Jack's will showed if anything happened where he could no longer care for himself, he would remain in his house until his death with whatever care needed to be done. They discharged him from the hospital and he went back home with round-the-clock care. He never left the house again after that incident.

"Jack hated God and blamed everyone around him for Victoria's death. Unlike Victoria, Jack viewed none of the cats as replacements for a child."

"So, what happened next? Did Jack live in the house until he died?"

"Jack developed other health issues later on. He ended up confined to bed and grieved himself to death over losing Victoria. He died in 1999 at eighty."

"And, no one else has lived in the house since his death?"

"Not according to our records. No one would buy the place. I think people were afraid Jack would hunt them down from beyond the grave with his shotgun loaded and aimed right at them."

I went on and asked Jace another question. "Jace, do you have any relatives in Mumford or know of anyone who owns a business there by the name of Madame Tallulah?"

"Well, yes, as a matter-of-fact, I do. She would be my Aunt Tallulah. She's a psychic medium. Why do you ask?"

"I met your Aunt Tallulah in Mumford while trying to get answers about the house."

"Well, I hope you got the answers you were looking for," said Jace as he escorted me to the door.

I left the Municipal Building, overwhelmed by my conversation with Jace. I could confirm that Madame Tallulah was his relative. I knew he shared the same square jaw and blue eyes like her. It must have been a family trait passed on to the next generation.

Madame Tallulah and Jace must have shared information about our home with each other in the past, before our family ever moved there. That's how Madame Tallulah knew about Jack, the cemetery on the grounds, and the spirits inside and outside the house. Even though I only mentioned the town I lived in, Madame Tallulah knew exactly which house. Was there anyone who didn't know about our home and its haunted past? Brock and I should have asked more questions before we bought it.

Victoria was Tori. Jack wrote her name on the mirror in the bathroom, but why? She died in the house, but her spirit was not in our home, only Jack's. It was not clear whether Jack died in our house or if he left the house when his health declined and died at a hospital. All I know is Jack's spirit was still inside our home, which explained his appearance to Max.

Jack had served in WWII, which explained the tin cup and the initials JA. But Sergeant Hernandez mentioned the grenade was from the Civil War Era. Why was a Civil War hand grenade buried on our property? Now I knew it wasn't Jack's. Was this proof a cemetery existed on our land? Who was the owner of the grenade?

When I got home, I would need to follow up with Brock on any information the college librarian found. I only hoped she had the answers.

CHAPTER SIX

The meeting with Jace Stephen raced through my mind. Jack was an actual person who lived and possibly died in our home. He obviously had mental and physical health issues from his service in WWII and the house fire that took the lives of his beloved wife Victoria and their cat, Sam. He was not in his right mind until his death. What did Jack want from our family, specifically from me?

The evening sun had set after dinner and the kids were unwinding in the basement as they watched television. Brock and I headed to our bedroom, sat down, and talked. I informed him of the information Ming Choo and Jace Stephen shared with me today. Brock was in shock about the details on Jack and that his wife's name was Victoria or Tori.

"Wow, that's hard to believe. Max really saw Jack. It's hard to wrap my mind around it. An actual spirit spoke with our son and wrote a name on our bathroom mirror. I'm glad you made a copy of the deed. Seeing both of their names in writing makes this more real."

"I know. I'm in shock about this, too," I said, rubbing the tense area on the side of my neck.

Brock shared some more interesting news that tied in to what Jace mentioned about our property.

"I spoke with Linda in the library about the hand grenade and what Sergeant Hernandez had mentioned about it being from the Civil War. She did some research and found a book from the Civil War Era dated 1861 to 1865. Inside the book were pictures of grenade types used during that time period. Our grenade matched the picture in the book." Brock showed me a photo on his phone.

"So, that definitely confirms it wasn't Jack's grenade from WWII. Jace Stephen said that Jack built this house on top of an old run-down cemetery. Could it have been a grenade from a soldier buried on our property? Maybe the one in my dream?" I asked anxiously.

"That could be possible. I'll check with Linda tomorrow to confirm burial ground sites in the Cedarville area. The spirit of whoever they buried on this property may be mad at Jack for building here, and now a curse is on this house."

"Do you think the black mist in the picture is a result from that curse?"

"I'm not sure, but it seems to fit what we're finding out about this place."

"Why is Jack making his presence known inside our house?"

"I believe we're caught in the middle of a spirit battle between the dead soldiers on this property and dead Jack in this house. The soldiers want the house removed from the burial ground. Jack wants the house to stay, and he doesn't want us living here."

"So, you're believing in the paranormal? I knew you would come around," I said with a smile. "By the way, there's a psychic medium named Madame Tallulah who I spoke with last Saturday. Our spirit situation required another opinion. I didn't tell you sooner because I was waiting to see what Ming Choo and Jace Stephen could tell me."

"I hope going to the psychic gave you the answers you were looking for. Did she tell you anything specific on your visit?"

"Madame Tallulah confirmed what we had already pieced together. Then come to find out, she's the aunt of Jace Stephen, the Municipal Building Commissioner. She probably already knew all about the house beforehand, and then I went and paid her for it."

"So, you were a sucker for her tall tales?"

"I guess you could say that. I'm so gullible."

At that moment, King sat up on the rug in our bedroom and looked over at the doorway. Next, he moved his head slowly, as if he had seen someone walk across the room. He stood on all four legs, stiffened his body and lowered his head in attack mode, and growled as he showed his sharp teeth. His head stopped moving as he stared at the entrance to our bathroom doorway. After that, his body relaxed and he no longer growled. Finally, King lay back down on the rug to rest as if nothing had happened.

"Hey, King, what's wrong? Everything's okay. You're a good boy." I leaned down to pat his head.

"What was that all about?" asked Brock.

"I have no clue," I said, confused by what just happened. This was a different reaction from King than his typical barking when the light flickered. He reacted defensively. What had he seen that made him upset enough to prepare himself for attack?

CHAPTER SEVEN

I t was two-thirty when the bus dropped off the kids after a busy day at school. Brock came home early from work and would watch the kids while I went back to visit Jace Stephen at the Municipal Building. I needed to find out more information on Jack and Victoria Aster. Jace was a great resource, since his grandmother and Victoria were best friends many years ago.

Before contacting Jace, I had followed up with the historical society in town showing them the house title and copy of the original deed, with Jack and Victoria's names. Their archives showed a map and photos of the property, similar to what Jace had already shown me. I checked an online database since Jack and Victoria were prominent figures in town with their construction company. The information wasn't anything new that Jace hadn't already shared. What I was most interested in was more about Jack and Victoria's life inside the house. Maybe this would help me figure out why Jack's spirit was still there.

Back at the Municipal Building, the administrative assistant escorted me to Jace's office. He was expecting my visit and motioned me to have a seat.

Jace began the conversation by sharing that Jack and Victoria met in high school, dated in college, and got married in 1940. Jack's father died unexpectedly that same year, left Jack the Westview

Lane property along with his construction company, and his life savings. Jack took over his father's business with Victoria by his side and changed the name to JV Construction Company, with Victoria as his partner. Their first year in business was going well, and they were expecting their first child. Everything fell into place with a new home, new business, and new family.

One day, when Victoria was eight months pregnant and Jack was off at work, she headed to the basement to do laundry. Their first cat, Leo, got spooked by a noise and ran in front of Victoria. She lost her balance and fell down the basement steps. Jack had come home for lunch and found Victoria passed out at the base of the stairway. She had blood from a head wound and blood down her leg. They took her to the nearest hospital in Cedarville. Victoria lost their baby boy and had to have a partial hysterectomy. They could never have children. After that, Jack hated God and cats even more than he already had. Victoria still loved Leo until the day he died. She always remained faithful in attendance at St. Elias Catholic Church and had not blamed God or anyone else for her loss. She had multiple cats throughout the coming years. Before one cat died, another cat was there to replace it. Cats were the children she could never have, and they were all male cats in memory of the son she had lost. Even though Jack wasn't happy about the cat, he loved Victoria and knew she needed to have a cat to fill that void in her life.

"I can't imagine the pain Victoria felt in her heart at the loss of their child. It also explains why there was children's wallpaper in Max's room," I said empathizing.

"Well, it went downhill from there," replied Jace.

Jace reported that Jack reacted differently in his grief. He became bitter towards God and other people because of the loss of their only child, his son, his future heir to the company. The next year, WWII needed more men and Jack got drafted and wasn't too happy about this. He made sure his Last Will and Testament were updated before his deployment. Jack used his service as an outlet for his anger towards God for everything he and his wife had been through. While Jack was in the war, he got injured and his mental status worsened over the years. As a precaution, Victoria took Jack with her to the construction site to monitor him and keep the business afloat. She finally sold JV Construction Company in 1984 and retired. Victoria was Jack's sole caretaker, and she needed to stay with him for his own safety.

"By the time 1998 rolled around, Victoria and Jack still lived in their home. As I mentioned the other day, Jack accidentally put gasoline in the wood burning kitchen stove, resulting in the explosion that killed Victoria and their last cat, Sam. Jack could not stand being without Victoria and died the following year in 1999. He had no funeral or burial site. He was not a believer in God."

"What did they do with Jack's body?" I asked.

"You may need to follow-up with the local funeral home. They're the only one around here to plan for dead bodies."

I thanked Jace for the detailed information. It filled in the blanks from what he had told me about Jack and Victoria on my first visit to see him.

After I left Jace, I stopped by and saw Mr. Oakland at Bluestone Funeral Home downtown. When I arrived, I asked Mr. Oakland if Jack Aster had an official burial site and where that might be. I wasn't sure if he died in the house or someone buried him on the property. Mr. Oakland checked his records. Upon his death, the funeral home cremated Jack Aster's body. In Jack's last will and testament, he requested his ashes scattered around the outside perimeter of the house. The funeral director, Mr. Wallace, followed through on Jack's last request.

"That seems rather odd, don't you think?" I asked.

"No, it's not unusual. Some people want to stay where they lived. Spreading their ashes on the property is one way of achieving this last wish. Jack attached himself to that house. Is there anything else I could help you with?"

"No. You've answered my question. Thank you for your time today."

Next, I headed over to the real estate office to see Ayesha Taylor and hoped I could gather more background information on our home. Ayesha was not aware of Jack's will that he left behind, and she had never seen it. The town attorney handled that document upon Jack's death and had it archived. Only he or his predecessor had the right to access it. Ayesha informed me that after Jack died, there was no other family to hand the house over to, so the town attorney and local real estate company would be responsible for the sale of the home.

"There were rumors about the haunting of the house, but no proof of this ever existed. It was only hearsay around town," said Ayesha.

"Did anyone from the real estate agency or the town's attorney office ever stay in the house?"

"No, not that I'm aware of. Why do you ask?"

"It might have confirmed whether the rumors were true. If they were, the real estate agency could have rethought the sale of the home and property to a family or at least make them aware of it."

"I see what you mean. There are some people who don't believe in spirits or the supernatural. I'll admit, I'm skeptical. So, it wouldn't matter to them about a rumor floating around town. It's something the buyer would need to determine or question on their own before purchasing the house and property and settling down there. It's not in the best interest of the real estate company to share a rumor that has no merit."

I would not tell Ayesha about our spirit encounters during this conversation. I wanted to wait until Brock and I were absolutely ready to uproot our family to another home. Ayesha just said that she hadn't believed in the rumors about the house being haunted, so anything I might add to that wouldn't have changed her mind.

"I'll talk with our company manager about your suggestion, Remi, in case there are any other ghosts roaming around in one of our homes that we have for sale," Ayesha said with a wink and a smile.

I thanked Ayesha for her time and headed back to the van. As I drove back home, all the information I had gathered today felt like pieces of a puzzle being put together. After twenty years of vacancy, our family came along and bought the house on Westview Lane. And the story of Jack's spirit in the house had begun. Out of all the homes to choose from with the pictures Ayesha had sent to Raheem, we chose this home. Somehow Brock and I became lured by it. Had we chosen this home to live in, or had this home really chosen me?

CHAPTER EIGHT

A t five-years-old, I had a sense for the afterlife. Was this the reason Max could see Jack? Did he inherit this ability to connect with a spirit entity from me? I was not aware back then, as I was now, of my gift. Or was it a curse? How was it possible for a Christian to connect with the dead?

I recalled my dream that started as a child and it became more repetitive and changed as the years went by. I was in my bedroom and woke up around three o'clock in the morning from a sound sleep. I remembered sensing something in the room and looked over toward the doorway. The bedroom door was closed, and I saw what appeared to be a man as he sat on the ground outside in an empty field. The picture was slightly blurry in my mind as I tried to remember that far back, but I could tell he had a sad expression on his face. His clothes were gray and resembled the uniform of a soldier against a darkened sky. The dirt on the ground was all around his body. It covered his face and arms, which created a mask that distorted his features. A large hole was in the ground beside the man. That dream haunted me through my childhood and into my adult years. I couldn't get the field, the man, his gray clothes, and dirt out of my mind. This was the same dream I had before we moved to Cedarville, only darker.

Now that we were in our home on Westview Lane, the details of my dream had changed. The darkness grew heavier and the background image and man were more difficult to visualize. Could this man be the soldier buried on our property under this house? Had King dug up this soldier's grenade? Was this the underlying reason we purchased this home? If so, what did this man want from me?

Brock called me from work today. He said he had met with the librarian regarding the Civil War burial sites in Cedarville.

"Linda had to dig pretty deep to get the information I requested." Brock reported that it seemed our home property was indeed a burial site for Civil War soldiers. The cemetery had become decayed through the years, and there was no follow-up to maintain the property.

"The city didn't confirm until after the Asters built the house that a cemetery was underneath it," said Brock.

"So, our house is sitting on top of a Civil War historical landmark?" I asked.

"Yes, that would be the case."

"Jace mentioned that Jack didn't care about this house standing on top of a cemetery. Did Linda find out any names of soldiers who might be buried on our land?"

"She didn't have any names, but she did mention they may be from Cherokee descent originating from North Carolina."

"Why would their graves be in Virginia?"

"Linda mentioned that some Cherokee's who served in the Civil War migrated to Virginia after the war."

"My mom has Cherokee on her side of the family. I can check with her later this weekend about ancestors who served during the

Civil War Era."

The information Linda shared with Brock had almost confirmed my childhood dream. The soldier who sat in the field surrounded by dirt was possibly on this exact property. That's why it looked familiar in the photo at the courthouse, and why it felt like déjà vu when we arrived at the house back in July. I needed to put a name with a face, and I hoped my mom could shed some light on this mystery soldier who haunted my dreams.

It was eight o'clock at night and time for the kids to head to bed. There was always playful banter between Dex, Londyn, and Nox. Who would beat whom up the basement steps? We had done the three Bs routine every night with bath, brush, and bed. The kids knew the drill well. Once in bed, Brock read them a quick story, they said prayers, and lights went out. No talking, no whispering, no giggling, just go to sleep. I checked in on Max, who was already in bed fast asleep since seven o'clock.

Brock and I watched television for a couple of hours before he took King out in the backyard briefly. Upon their return, King came back to our room and lay down on the rug. By the time Brock and I crawled under the covers, it was ten o'clock. Everything that occurred since we moved into our house exhausted us. What else could happen?

Just as Brock and I had settled in bed and everything was quiet, a strange sensation occurred at my feet.

"Brock," I whispered as I gave him a nudge.

"Hm, what?" asked Brock, half asleep.

"I feel something in the bed."

"What? I was almost asleep, Remi. What do you mean something's in the bed? Maybe it's me you feel."

"Shh, be quiet for one second. Lay perfectly still."

"I'm laying still."

"Do you feel it?"

"What am I supposed to be feeling?"

"It feels like something's walking on top of the covers at our feet with a step, step, step motion. Now, it's moving up the bed in between us. Do you feel it, now?"

Brock paused for a moment and then said, "Yes, now I feel it. What do you think it is?"

"It feels like a small animal. It's not heavy like a dog, but light like a cat," I said with a gasp. "Jace said that Jack and Victoria had a cat that she loved like a child. His name was Sam. Do you think it may be ghost cat Sam in our bed? He died in the house fire with her."

"Anything is possible, as long as it doesn't attack us in our sleep."

"That's not funny, Brock. Do you think ghost cat Sam is what King saw in our room that made him growl, or do you think it was Jack?"

"Who knows what King may have seen."

"Now, I won't be able to go to sleep."

"Remi, stop worrying. You need your rest," said Brock as he reached over to hug and kiss me, then turned on his right side to sleep.

While Brock dozed off, I continued to lie there and wondered why a dead cat had visited our bed tonight. How was it possible to feel something as it walked on our bed but not see anything? What did ghost cat Sam want?

CHAPTER NINE

The weather started getting cooler outside as we eased into December. One Saturday morning, Dex, Londyn, Nox, and Max were all up early. King sat by the kitchen table as I prepared a pancake breakfast. It was the one food item the kids all agreed to eat. Brock came in and sat with us. We ate breakfast as a family, unlike the chaotic weekday mornings in our home. We made casual conversation at the table. Did everyone sleep well? What was everyone planning to do today? It was at that moment when Nox spoke up.

"Something was in my bed last night," said Nox.

"Yeah, what he said," chimed Dex and Londyn.

"Me too," said Max as he copied his siblings.

"Whoa, wait a minute. Nox spoke first. So Nox, tell us what was in your bed last night," I said attentively.

"I have no clue. I couldn't see it. I felt it."

"Well, what did you feel?"

"I know what it was," interrupted Dex.

"Dex, let your brother talk. Go ahead, Nox."

"Well, something crawled at my feet and behind my back. I jumped out of bed and flipped the covers off, but nothing was there."

"Yeah, he came into my bedroom and tried to crawl in the bed with me. I told him I felt something in my bed," said Dex.

"Then, they tried to crawl in bed with me. I told them I felt something in my bed, too. What do you think it was, Mom and Dad?" asked Londyn.

Brock and I stared at each other in disbelief. It still haunted me by the ghost-like creature who inhabited our bed last night. Now, this thing or spirit invaded our children's beds. Dex interrupted before Brock and I could respond to the question Londyn asked.

"The three of us got together and slept on the floor in Max's room. He was still asleep, so we figured nothing bothered him and we would be safe there," said Dex.

"I know our bedroom is further away, but I should've heard each of you running around in your rooms," I said with concern, as I walked over and gave each of them a hug.

"We were running on our tippy-toes, covering our mouths trying not to scream, and whispering with each other in the room about what happened. We didn't want to wake up Max and make him afraid," Dex said with compassion, looking over at his sister and brothers.

"Why didn't you wake us up?" I wondered.

"We thought about coming downstairs to tell you, but we were okay and decided to just go in Max's room," Dex reassured with such maturity.

"How are each of you feeling this morning after what happened?" Brock asked as he gave each of the kids a hug, too.

"We're better now," said Londyn as she finished up her breakfast.

"We're the four musketeers and tough when we're together," said Nox with a big grin.

"They're right. Everything's okay. I just hope whatever that feeling was in bed never comes back," said Dex, looking relieved it was over.

"I hope whatever it was doesn't come back either. Just remember that Mom and Dad are here when you need us. Don't feel you have to be so brave you don't need our help anymore. Okay?" asked Brock.

"Okay," chimed all four kids.

"Now that everyone finished breakfast, why don't each of you go outside and play in the backyard. Supervise your baby brother and take King, too. Maybe we can go to the mall later today," I said with a hint of excitement.

"Yay, the mall," cheered all four kids.

The children got up from the table, turned on the basement light, and hurried down the steps to get their winter coats, hats, and gloves on. Max went down the steps as I followed behind. I got Max bundled up and then Dex took him by the hand and they went out the basement door to play. King ran out the door after them.

I headed back upstairs where Brock and I finished cleaning up the kitchen. We sat back down at the table, relaxed, read the paper, and drank our coffee. At that moment, we heard a clanging sound in the basement.

"Hey, did one of you kids forget something?" I loudly asked. There was no response. I looked over at Brock, and the noise from the basement started again.

"What's that sound?" I asked, unsure of what I heard.

"It sounds like my tools are being moved on the workbench," Brock said with a confused look on his face.

Brock got up from his chair and looked out the back window. All four children were outside playing whiffle ball while King chased after them in the yard. In the basement, a tool from the workbench fell onto the floor. Brock stood at the top of the basement steps and the light flickered. I quickly reached for a knife in the silverware drawer and handed it to Brock.

"Here, Brock, take this with you for safety."

"Gee, thanks, honey. A butter knife will show whoever's in the basement that I mean business."

"Wait right there," I said as I hurriedly ran up the steps and back down with Dex's baseball bat and handed it to Brock.

Brock slowly started down the basement staircase with the bat positioned and ready to swing. Whoever or whatever was down there would be frightened away just by the sheer noise Brock made with each heavy step. Once he reached the bottom, he leaned over and turned on the overhead light to the workbench area.

"What's there, Brock?"

"Come on down and see for yourself."

I headed down the basement stairs and over to where Brock stood at his workbench. I could sense a presence in the basement with us. It felt like we were being watched. There was a change in the surrounding air in that space.

"I smell cigarettes down here and it is freezing right where I'm standing." I rubbed both of my upper arms. "But the heat's on." I stretched my hand up near the vent on the back wall and felt the warm air as it came out. "Do you smell the smoke or feel the coldness, Brock?"

"No, I don't smell or feel anything like that. But look at my workbench."

Brock's tools on his workbench board pulled loose from one corner, causing some tools to fall. A wrench was on the concrete floor.

"How did that happen?" I asked.

"I don't know," said Brock.

"You don't think the kids pulled it loose playing with the tools, do you?"

"No, everything was fine when I checked into the basement last night. Nothing was out of place. You were just down here earlier when the kids got their coats to go outside. No one touched the workbench area."

"Wait, do you smell something else?" I asked, raising my nose up, sniffing the air. "This time I'm not talking about the cigarette odor. It smells like something died," I said, feeling nauseous from the scent. "That smell was not down here earlier."

"No, I smell nothing. Does it smell like the sewer from the bathroom?"

"It has a pungent odor. How can you not smell it?" I asked, as I looked at Brock with a puzzled glance. "Let me see if I can track down where it's coming from."

I followed the path of this obnoxious odor as I used my nose as a guide and sniffed out every square inch of the basement. The odor wasn't coming from the bathroom where Brock had suggested it might be. It seemed to be much stronger as I got closer to the drain in the concrete floor. I slowly bent down to put my nose closer to the drain opening. Immediately, I pulled my head back and gagged. "It's right here, Brock. What's that smell?"

Brock leaned down towards the drain, sniffed once, and said, "I'm sorry, honey. I really smell nothing. Maybe a rodent got into our drain line. I'll have to call a plumber to see if we have any cracks or openings in the line. We can't do anything until Monday."

"I've got my phone. I'll make a note right now. This house is worrying me. I don't like that our children are being affected by a spirit in the house. I think we need to start looking for another place to live. I don't think Jack's spirit likes us being here."

"I'm agreeing with you. We definitely need to look around for other houses. We'll need to contact Ayesha soon to start the process."

"I'll follow up with my mother right now to see if there's any chance this property is connected to our Cherokee family roots."

I had my cell phone in my hand as I dialed my mom. After quick greetings, I told her I had some questions about her Cherokee ancestry. She explained to me her ancestors came from North Carolina before they migrated to Virginia to settle down. My third great-grandfather who was a Cherokee, named Jake Awahili, donned a Confederate uniform and fought in the Civil War. As mom recalled from stories told by her parents, Grandpa Jake wanted to fight on the Union side to support freeing the slaves. But transportation during that time was insufficient and the travel too intense for him to switch sides. He had to stay where he had volunteered when he signed up. According to Mom, Grandpa Jake lived in Cedarville after the war. He remained there until his death and they buried his body with other Civil War soldiers, but they did not find the gravesite. After the call ended, I wondered if my

Grandpa Jake had been the soldier in my childhood dream. If so, what did he need from me?

Meanwhile, Brock brought the kids and King back inside for a quick snack before we left for the mall. We loaded up our family on both sides of the van and took King with us. As I opened the passenger side door, I felt someone's eyes watching me from inside the house. When I looked back, I thought I saw a dark figure in the upstairs hall window, but it quickly disappeared. Maybe it was just my imagination playing tricks on me. But then, I remembered Ayesha's husband detected something in that same window, and Brock caught sight of a figure in Max's bedroom window. It seemed peculiar what each had seen on separate occasions. Now I recognized the very same thing.

Just then, a black mist formed above the house. I gasped, as my mind had a flashback to my dream with darkness over my head and being chased. My breathing increased, and my heart raced. I quickly got into the van and kept quiet about what I saw so Brock and the children wouldn't be frightened. I looked back out the van window at the black mist as it lingered in the air. This was not a potential storm. Now, I knew there was evil living inside our home and surrounded by evil on the outside as well. Was this the evil that chased me in my dream? I needed to protect our family from this vile entity before something serious happened. The only way I could accomplish this would be to move our family out.

"Remi, are you okay?" asked Brock, as he reached over and gently touched my arm.

I leaned over and whispered in Brock's right ear to look out the window at the house. I informed him the black mist was back and so was the figure in the window. Brock immediately stepped out of the van for a better view.

When he got back inside the van, he said, "I see nothing. Whatever was there left. Are you sure you still want to go to the mall?"

"Yes, I'll be fine. The kids are looking forward to it. We can talk more about it later," I replied. I thought about my mantra, "You can do this, Remi, just breathe" as I took a deep breath in and slowly exhaled. My breathing and heart slowed down.

I turned to look out the car window again and the black mist was gone, as Brock had mentioned. I knew this wasn't my imagination. What was the meaning of this black mist? Had Jack been the figure who stood in the upstairs hallway window and the window in Max's room and stared at us with his evil eyes all this time?

CHAPTER TEN

The December sun had set and the air temperature plummeted. We arrived back home from the mall, the kids bathed, and we all got ready for bed. Afterward, Brock and I sat down in our room to relax.

"What do you think the black mist and the figure in the window mean?" I asked, feeling tense.

"I'm not sure. We already know there's some kind of spirit battle outside and inside this house and property. An evil force is still lingering around." Brock had an air of concern in his voice.

"Do you think something bad will happen?"

"I don't know what will happen, Remi. We need to sell this house and never look back."

I was glad Brock agreed with me about moving out. We weren't sure how the house would sell since Jack lived here and was a spirit obsessed with this place and our family's presence. Somehow, I thought Ayesha was already aware from past rumors about the spirits, but she didn't have proof of specific encounters, neither had she believed in them. We would contact Ayesha and have the house placed on the market in January for an early jump-start towards the spring home sales rush.

Brock and I were sound asleep in bed when suddenly, a crying sound startled me awake. I turned my head. The time was three o'clock. Was Max awake or did he have a bad dream? I felt drowsy, but got out of bed. At that very moment, I heard footsteps on the staircase. Who was going up the steps at this hour? Was it one of the other kids?

By the time I reached our bedroom doorway, I no longer heard Max cry. As I tiptoed past the living room and got closer to the staircase, I smelled stale cigarette smoke and felt a cool sensation in the room. I went up the steps to Max's room at a brisk pace. The door to his room was not closed.

That's odd, I thought. I always secured his door when he slept to keep out the rest of the noise in the house.

I could see Max as he sat in his bed with a straw drinking cup. The rocking chair moved back and forth, but no one sat there. The cigarette odor and coolness were both strong in Max's room. How in the world was this chair rocking? I reached out and touched the chair, and it stopped moving. The cigarette odor and coolness quickly left.

"Max, how did you get that drink?" I asked in a soft whisper.

"Jack," said Max, with his eyes half closed and looking drowsy.

"Jack brought you a drink?"

"Yeah, Jack," said Max as he finished his drink and handed the cup to me. I got Max up, took him to the bathroom, and came back to his room. The rocking chair remained still, so I took Max and rocked him back to sleep. I placed him on his bed, covered him with his blanket, and quietly closed the door.

What just happened in there? I took a deep breath, and I checked in on Dex, Londyn, and Nox. Their bedroom doors had remained closed. I opened each door, and the children were fast asleep in their beds. Why did Jack always bother Max?

"Jack, you are freaking me out. Leave my children alone, especially Max!" I angrily whispered, tightening my jaw as I clenched my teeth and shook my fist in the air.

I went back downstairs and into the kitchen. There was no way I could go back to sleep, so I fixed myself a cup of hot chamomile tea in the microwave. I got the two-step ladder from the hall closet and grabbed the magnet box hidden on the back of the refrigerator. There was a locked cabinet above the sink where I kept a bottle of bourbon. I added a splash or two or maybe three to my tea. I needed something to take the edge off my fears and this house. Wine was no longer enough to calm my nerves with Jack around.

I took my cup and went back upstairs. I opened Max's door and he was sound asleep. I set my tea down on the dresser, went into the hallway, and entered Dex's room. I got his bat off the wall rack and took it with me to Max's room. I sat in the rocking chair with the bat in my lap as I slowly sipped my enhanced cup of tea. I couldn't help but think how Jack had become more brazen in his attempt to keep a reign on this house and our family. What was he up to? He annoyed me as he attempted to interfere with Max. He opened the bedroom door, rocked in his chair, and gave Max a straw cup with water. Madame Tallulah had said that a child could see a spirit because it had not deceived his mind or something to that effect. Had Jack done what Max needed because I hadn't responded to his cries quick enough? Or did he use Max to get closer to me?

Jace had mentioned that Jack and Victoria could not have children, and how much he hated the cat. Did Jack try to get close to Max because he had lost his own child? Max was vulnerable and open-minded to his presence. It seemed Jack took advantage of this. Would he ever hurt Max?

I finished my tea and felt the effects of the bourbon. My eyes felt heavy as I sat in the rocking chair and drifted off to sleep. The morning rush and busy routine with the kids would start again in a few more hours. After what happened with Max tonight, I would not allow Jack to use my child or any of my children as a pawn in his spirit world game. The next time I would be ready for Jack, more than ready as I squeezed the bat tightly in my hands.

CHAPTER ELEVEN

The next morning, I had a slight hangover from the enhanced drink and lack of proper sleep. I told Brock, before he left for work, about what had happened with Max last night. First, I explained to him how I heard Max cry. There was the sound of footsteps on the staircase. Then, Max said the name 'Jack' when I asked him who brought the straw cup. I informed Brock the rocking chair moved back and forth, but no one was there.

"I didn't realize all of that happened. When the alarm went off, you weren't in bed. I thought you had gone to check on Max, or one of the other kids, or couldn't sleep and went elsewhere to read. I didn't know you sat up in the rocking chair the rest of the night in Max's room. You look exhausted," said Brock as he reached out his arms to hold me close.

I could smell his spice cologne and wanted to fall asleep right there in his arms and forget about what took place last night.

"Just keep holding me," I said with my head tucked under his chin.

"How's Max doing this morning?" asked Brock, concerned he hadn't seen him up yet.

"He's still asleep in his room. I'll get him up in a few minutes. The night was restless for both of us."

"How are you doing? I mean really doing."

"I want out of this house. I'm tired of dealing with a spirit you can't even see. I don't want him near our children."

"I'll get in touch with Ayesha to see where we are in terms of homes and getting this one on the market as soon as possible. Will you be okay today at the house with Max and King?"

"Yes, I'll be all right."

"Boy Scout promise you'll call if you need me," said Brock holding up his three fingers.

I smiled, held up three fingers, and said, "I Girl Scout promise."

Brock gave me a kiss and headed out the door to work. I smelled his cologne as it hung in the air after he left.

The kids had already gone to school. Max got up, ate breakfast, and went into the living room with King by his side as he played with his toys. I cleaned up the morning mess in the kitchen after breakfast. When I finished, I remembered I needed to contact the plumber about the dead animal smell in our basement. I had totally forgotten about the note on my phone to follow-up. When I called, they said they would send someone out next week.

Once my phone call ended, I went upstairs, gathered the dirty laundry, got Max and King from the living room, and we headed to the basement. Max watched television while King lay down on the rug to rest. I started the washing machine and ironed the clothes. Suddenly, I heard heavy footstep sounds above me, which came from the kitchen area. The floor creaked with each step that was made.

"Who's up there?" I exclaimed.

The footsteps stopped. There was no response. My hand reached down instinctively to the phone in my pocket. I turned off the iron and checked on Max and King. Max had laid his head down on King's body and both had fallen asleep on the rug.

I went to the staircase, and the footsteps started again. As I stomped up the steps towards the kitchen, the footsteps stopped. When I reached the top, I poked my head around the doorway. And no one was there. I looked around at the main level of the house in all the rooms, still no one. Then, I went upstairs to the children's bedrooms, and no one was there. After that, I went back down to the kitchen and noticed the tin cup wasn't at the sink. I looked around but couldn't find it. On a hunch, I got the two-step ladder from the hall closet, brought it to the kitchen, climbed up, and checked inside the cabinet. I pulled out the metal bread box on the top shelf in the far upper left corner. There it was, hidden inside where I had originally found it.

How did the tin cup get back in the bread box and cabinet? I wondered.

"Okay, Jack. Did you put this tin cup back in the cabinet? Why did you do that? This is not your house anymore. And I know you were in Max's room last night. Stay out of there. Max is not your child. He's my child! Do you hear me? How many times must I say it? Leave our family alone!" I retorted, looking around the room, waiting for Jack to appear.

I placed the tin cup back at the kitchen sink and left the breadbox in the cabinet. I took the two-step ladder and put it back in the hall closet. I headed down the steps to the basement to finish the rest of my ironing. Max and King were still in the rec room asleep. "I need to check with someone on how to get rid of spirits in this house or no one will ever want to live here," I muttered under my breath.

"Can you hear me, Jack? I'm going to get rid of you from our home if it's the last thing I do!" I said, shaking my fist in the air.

After the laundry finished, I decided I needed to take Max and get out of the house for a break while the other three kids were still at school. I called and joined a community-based parent support group near our town. It was an opportunity where parents could vent, share advice, and socialize with each other. The meeting was at the local Fit-4-All wellness center just outside the downtown area in Cedarville and was free to attend.

We arrived at a three-story white brick building on a street suitably named Fitness Lane. I looked up at the building, and through tinted glass I saw silhouettes of people exercising.

I took Max inside and introduced ourselves to the receptionist. She instructed us to wait in the lobby until the leader of the parent group and attendees all arrived, and we would head to the meeting room together.

While we waited, I grabbed a brochure at the front entrance desk. I wanted to see what kind of exercise class and child care they offered, just in case I might be interested in joining one day. I was never very good at sticking to a health program, especially at home.

Just then, I glanced up from the brochure and noticed that parents and children of the group meeting had trickled in the front door. The receptionist held up a parent group sign and gathered everyone together. Max and I followed behind them on the elevator to the room upstairs. I took Max to the play area in the room next door, and he immediately interacted with the other kids.

Each of the parents in our group sat on a folding chair in a circle and shared concerns about their children and their own personal life at home. Some of those issues were on adoption, child support, financial concerns, a grandparent raising her grandchild, divorced parents, death of a spouse, and foster care.

The information that was shared was a lot to process all at once. I wasn't aware before this meeting of what the other parents would discuss and to what extent.

Now it was my turn to share. My issues sounded trivial compared to the rest of the parent group. What would be the best way to approach my question about a spirit entity in the house?

"Hello, I'm Remi. I have three elementary school-aged children and one toddler at home. Our family just moved to Cedarville, and it's been a challenge settling in to our new home and adjusting to the changes. I'm feeling overwhelmed." That was an understatement. I didn't feel I could share the spirit part of my life, not if we wanted to sell our house. Would this group be able to handle that I had a ghost in my house, or would they think I was having a mental breakdown? Was there anyone I could trust in this group? Would they even believe me?

"Where's your house located?" asked Neco.

"We moved onto 119 Westview Lane," I said. Everyone in the room gasped and whispered amongst themselves after I announced my address. "What did I say? What was the gasping for?"

"You live in a haunted house," said Betty. "My sister Tammy went over there. She was thinking of buying the house to fix it up for resale. That's what she does for a living. When Tammy went inside, she said strange things happened. She heard clanging noises in the basement and footsteps in the upstairs hallway. She got spooked, ran out of the house, and never looked back."

"Yeah, I know someone who wanted to move there, too. He said it felt like someone was watching him from the window when he was standing outside the house. He saw no one. When he went in the house, the lights flickered whenever he turned on a switch. Then, he heard footsteps in the kitchen while he was upstairs, looking around. No one else was inside the house with him. The realtor was sitting outside in her car," said Amanda.

"I heard someone died in that house. That's why it's haunted," Ed commented.

"Do you know the name of the person who died in the house, Ed?" I asked.

"Yes, I believe it was a woman named Vicky, and a man named Jacob. It was something close to that."

"What about the name Jack and Victoria? Does that ring a bell?"

"Why yes, that sounds about right."

"Our family looked through the house when my husband was alive," said Sakura. "I remember hearing footsteps on the staircase and in the living room. I was the only one around when it happened. I told my husband, and we looked elsewhere. It felt creepy being there."

"I had a friend who worked for JV Construction. That was the homeowner's company. He said some workers went there to remove furniture after an estate sale and had a hard time opening the master bedroom door. When he got it opened, he went inside the room and the shower water was running and steam was on the mirror. He wasn't sure how that happened. He saw the letters T and O, then a vertical straight line appeared while he was standing there, as if another letter was being written. It freaked him out. He left and never returned," said Kris.

Danielle spoke up and said, "My mother had a friend who was clairvoyant. She has now passed, but she predicted the owner would die in that house and haunt it forever. She also said there were other spirits outside the house that would never leave as long as the dead owner's spirit remained inside."

Amber chimed in, saying, "My best friend told me her grandparents shared something with her about the house you live in. They had gone over there out of curiosity when the ghost rumors started floating around. My friend said her grandparents got spooked when the stove door opened up as they walked by. They also heard doors upstairs opening and closing. That was good enough for them to leave and never go back."

"Thanks everyone for letting me know," I said, feeling shocked by hearing so many stories.

Most parents in the group either had an occurrence in our house or knew of someone who had. Was Jack responsible for the same scare tactics these group members and their friends experienced as our family had? I should be grateful that this proved I wasn't crazy after all.

"I have a question to ask all of you. Why didn't anyone come by our house and share your spirit encounter with our family?" I asked, as the group members looked at each other.

Betty spoke up and said, "I guess I thought whoever bought the house already knew about its past. If I had known your family wasn't aware of the house, I would have driven straight up there to tell you myself about the ghost rumors being true."

Everyone else in the room shook their heads in agreement and murmured the words 'yeah' and 'right.'

There was more to Jack than clanging sounds, flickering lights, or words on a mirror. Had Jack scared off everyone interested in the house? Was our family meant to move there? I needed to find an expert on house cleansing who could answer my questions and calm my fears over our spirit intruder, just as Madame Tallulah suggested. That was next on my agenda, and I would start at the local library in town.

When I got up to leave the meeting, I headed towards the snack table at the back of the room to get a few items for Max and me to take home. A woman who was close to my age approached me. She was tall, slender, reddish-colored hair, and fair complexion.

"Hi, my name is Josephine. People call me Josie for short."

"Hi, Josie, my name is Remi, which is short for Remi," I said as we both laughed.

"So, did you enjoy the meeting?"

"Yes, there was an interesting mix of moms and dads here today. Some parents in the group could have used a family guidance counselor."

"I agree. Life can be stressful and throw some curves our way. Raising a child is hard enough. But I have a sense you weren't here for child rearing or family advice, am I right?"

"Josie, I came because the house we just moved into is proving to be more than I bargained for. It seems other people in the group knew more about my house than I did before our family moved here."

"Oh, where did you say you moved to again? I missed that part of the meeting to use the lady's room."

"Our family moved into the home on Westview Lane."

"Oh, you must be the Sterling family. We didn't say our last names at the meeting, so it never occurred to me you were the new family who just moved into that house."

"How did you know my last name?"

"Word spreads fast around here when someone new comes to our area. You moved into the old Aster house. I've heard it's haunted, too. I feel bad you have seen no neighbors since you moved into town. It might be they're afraid to step foot on the property from all the haunted house rumors. I should have reached out and attempted to see you."

"What story do you have to share about our house being haunted?"

"My grandparents went to church with one of the original owners. Her name was Victoria Aster. I believe she died in an explosion in the house. Her husband Jack would never leave the home, and I think he died there, too. That's why people say it's haunted."

"Do you know which room in the house Jack may have died?"

"I would assume his bedroom. He was incapacitated until his death, so I heard."

"Was Jack's bedroom upstairs or downstairs?"

"I would think it was on the main level somewhere. He couldn't go up and down steps in his last year of life."

"Someone else I recently met shared similar information on Jack and his wife. It was the Building Commissioner Jace Stephen. Do you know him?"

"Why yes, Jace is my brother. Our mom told us everything she learned from her mother about the Asters, their home, and life.

Victoria Aster and our grandmother were best friends. As far as their background, Jace knows way more than I do about the Aster home and their lives. Talk to him if you need more information. I'm sure he would be glad to tell you what you need to know, if it makes you feel any better."

"Wow, you're Jace's sister. I would never have put the two of you together as siblings."

"I know. He's all tanned and I'm pasty pale. Jace inherited my dad's side of the family genes, and I inherited my mother's. Go figure."

"I see a resemblance in your eyes and smile."

"It's a common trait in our family."

"Is everyone related around here? I met your Aunt Tallulah, too."

"Oh my, you met my mom's younger sister Aunt Tallulah? You really are desperate, aren't you?"

"Yes, I guess I am," I said, as we both laughed.

We walked out to our cars. "It was great talking with you, Josie. Maybe I'll see you at the next parent group meeting."

"So, you're coming back? Great, I'll see you next week. Here's my number if you need to talk or need help with a babysitter before our next group get-together. Maybe at the next meeting you could share one of your ghost stories with us," said Josie with a sly grin.

"I think at the next group meeting I'll ask for advice on how to handle my spirit problem and see what they come up with," I said with a smile.

Josie got into her car with her son, waved, and drove away. I was glad I came today. It felt good knowing that I could openly share my Jack encounters with the group.

What I needed to do was find out how to get rid of Jack. The local library would be next on my list for information on how to carry out this task. Hopefully, the librarian could recommend someone locally to provide the house cleansing service. Would there ever be anything to extract Jack's spirit from our home?

CHAPTER TWELVE

C hristmas 2019 was over and 2020 was upon us. Jack's spirit had kept a low profile during this week, which surprised me. I felt his presence throughout our home which made me uneasy that something might happen. His eyes watched us. Who knew what he might be up to. I had to keep my guard up while I looked over my shoulder and listened for any sign that Jack would be ready to frighten or harm our family. I was tense and less relaxed during this special time of the year, but I made sure Brock and the kids didn't see me this way. Christmas was a joyful time, and I wouldn't allow my fear of Jack to ruin it. I wondered if Jack hadn't liked Christmas because he was an atheist and the season centered on God's son and His birth. Was he offended by this celebratory holiday? Was this a reminder of the son he and Victoria lost and the unfairness of it all?

As the holiday was winding down, Brock and I went in the living room and sat quietly on the couch. We relaxed and read a book near the warmth of the fireplace. At that very moment, I detected a smell of stale cigarette smoke and coolness in the air. On the Christmas tree, the lights flickered, several blew out, sparks flew, and a paper nativity ornament ignited. That ornament was from the 1800s and a gift handed down to me from my Grandma Leona. She inherited it from her first great-grandparents, Jake and

Lilly. I rushed over to the ornament, which had fallen off the tree onto the floor, and used my fingers to snuff out the smoldering edge.

"Okay, Jack. I know you're in here. You've been lying low and watching us this whole time. Now, you've made me mad. That was my ornament and a family heirloom that belonged to my third great-grandfather and grandmother. Why did you do that, Jack? Don't touch what isn't yours. Leave us alone!" I retorted as I held the ornament delicately in my hand.

"I know how much that ornament means to you. Now Jack is targeting items that are personal to us." Brock reached over to give me a hug.

"When will this ever stop?"

"I don't have an answer for that. We'll be out of this house soon. Ayesha is working on finding our next home."

"I hope it'll be as far away as possible from this place."

At that very moment, the smell of cigarette smoke and cool sensation left the living room. All the Christmas tree lights had burned out and would need to be thrown away, thanks to Jack's meddling. Brock and I took down the Christmas decorations in the living room. What was it with this spirit and his intrusion into our personal space? Why would he single out that ornament on the tree to destroy and not the others?

After the holiday break, our family got back to our weekly routine. Today was Friday. The plumber and his assistant finally came to the house to follow up on the problem with the strange odor from the basement that would come and go. They apologized for the delay of their visit due to scheduling conflicts. The plumber checked the drain on the concrete floor as he placed a thin wire camera inside it. He also had done the same thing outside in the backyard where the water and sewer lines were located. There were no cracks, leaks, or dead rodents found. Everything looked fine. The odor wasn't noticeable today. Who knows what caused that awful smell the day Brock and I were in the basement. I was glad it did no damage to the drainage lines. It would have been more of an expense than we could handle with this house.

On Saturday, I seized the opportunity and headed to the public library downtown. I needed to find some information on spirit cleansing and anyone who might perform this ritual. It would be a chance for me to have some alone time, too.

The library's red brick building sat on a small corner lot on Luck Avenue. It was one level with clear glass windows in front. You could see directly inside at the shelves of books on display. The bright, warm sunshine streamed through the windows where they arranged chairs for reading. When I entered the building, I smelled fresh coffee at the coffee bar area and could not resist, so I stopped to get a cup.

Coffee and books what a brilliant combination, I thought.

Afterward, I walked over to the receptionist's desk and spoke with the librarian on duty.

"Hi Nadia, my name is Remi. I'm looking for information on spirit cleansing. Could you point me to the right section?"

"Certainly, Remi, let me walk you over there instead and show you what books we have available. Are you having a problem with a spirit entity?"

"Well, let's just say I'm preparing myself in the event I need to take action."

Nadia escorted me to the section at the back of the library under Religion and Spiritual Healing before she went back to assist another customer. As I rummaged through the books, I noticed several had mentioned smudging to cleanse the home of negative energy.

The cleansing required a bowl that had sage in it, a lighter or match used to burn it, a feather that would waft the burning sage through the air in the house, and a window left open for the negative energy to escape. Sea salt was an option and placed in the corners of the room to absorb the negative energy. Crystals were a shield of protection to either wear or have placed in the doorway inside the home. A smudge prayer would need to be said during the cleansing, as a way of letting the spirit know it was time to leave. I think I had seen someone on television do a similar smudging technique on one of those medium shows.

I would need to find a professional to perform the cleansing. Nadia was very helpful and referred me to a Cherokee Native American Shaman in town. I left the library and drove to the Indigenous Center near Jamestown University. The facility was in a gray stone building with oak wooden doors and clear glass windows. I parked outside in the visitor space and entered the building. A gentleman by the name of Diwali introduced himself to me. He inquired about our home situation and set up a one hour appointment to do our house cleansing on Wednesday the following week.

Jack's spirit had become more irritated on the days that led up to Diwali's visit. I had previously warned Jack to leave us alone, and he ignored me. His spirit slammed the tools on the workbench in the basement. He paced heavily on the kitchen floor while I tried to rest in the bedroom. He took one of my favorite coffee cups from the kitchen counter and threw it on the floor, which broke into little pieces.

I couldn't take much more and got Max and King into the van and left the house. We went to a local park. I called Brock at work and left him a voice message about what had happened. I drove back home when it was time for the kids to return from school.

Brock called back and said, "Remi, let me stay home with you until Diwali completes the cleansing process. I don't want to risk Jack hurting you or Max."

"No, it's okay. I'll be fine. Jack might scare me, but he can't control me."

"I can get someone else to cover my classes. Let me be there for you."

"You are here for me, Brock. Whenever you hold me close and give me a hug nothing else matters in that moment."

"Then, the next time I hold you, I won't let you go. I'll leave work early today and come home right now."

When Brock arrived at the house, he came inside, walked straight towards me, and wrapped his muscular arms around my body. The tension melted away. It was exactly what I needed.

Wednesday arrived. The kids were at school, and Diwali would come to the house at twelve o'clock. I called Josie to see if she could babysit Max during Diwali's visit, but she wasn't available. As my last resort, I called Brock at the college in between his classes, and he agreed to watch Max while on his extended lunch break. I loaded up the van with Max and headed to Jamestown University. Brock's office was on the third floor. His door was open, and he finished his phone call as Max and I headed inside.

"Thanks for doing this, Brock. I'm not sure what Diwali's procedure will be. I didn't want Max in the way."

"Good news! I just got off the phone and could find a substitute who can take over my one-thirty class. I'll keep Max with me. Let me know when Diwali completes the cleansing, and Max and I will head back to the house."

"That'll be great!" I gave Brock a kiss and headed back out.

Diwali arrived at our home on time. He got out of his car, stood there in our driveway for a while, and didn't move. He certainly dressed himself for the occasion in his Native American ceremonial attire. He wore a suede light brown shirt with fringe on the sleeves, matching pants, and detailed moccasin boots with turquoise and white beads. His black hair fell loosely past his shoulders and large silver looped earrings glistened in the sun. He carried a brown leather bag over his left shoulder. I stood at the open front door and Diwali acknowledged me with a wave. He went to the back of the house to look around. Finally, he came to the front door of our home.

"Hello, Diwali," I said.

"Ma'am, there seems to be an evil presence emanating from your house. I can see darkness overhead as a black mist. I also sense spirits behind your house, and they may be the reason for the black mist," said Diwali.

"I know. I've seen the dark mist in pictures of the house. And I saw it the other day when our family went out for a trip to the mall. It comes and goes. The Building Commissioner Jace Stephen said this house is built on top of a Civil War burial site. What do you think it all means?"

"Evil lives here inside and outside your house. That is what it means. If there are dead soldiers on this property, they may have cast a curse on the house when the original owner built it. The spirits of the soldiers buried here may want the house gone, now that the owner has died. The black mist will remain as long as the house still stands. I will see what I can do but no promises."

"Yes, of course. I understand. Please come in."

"May I look around inside your house before I get started?"

"Yes, help yourself."

As Diwali entered our home, he lingered in the hallway, headed up the steps to the children's rooms, came back downstairs through the rooms on the main level, and went down into the basement. After he had toured the house, Diwali went back toward the master bedroom a second time.

"This is where evil lives."

"What do you mean?"

"I can feel the spirit's evil presence in your bedroom stronger than anywhere else in the house. Do you know if someone died in this room?"

"No, not exactly. I don't have any proof regarding that question, only hearsay. But our son, Max, met the entity in this house. His name is Jack."

"Your child is young in mind and spirit. He is not aware of the difference between good and evil. The spirit entity in the house is taking advantage of your son's child-like faith, and he may try to get to you by using your son instead. Keep alert. Let me get started with the cleansing right away."

Diwali reached inside of his shoulder bag for his supplies. He took out his crystals and placed them in the master bedroom and front doorways. Next, he placed sea salt in the corners of the bedroom and opened a window for the negative energy to escape as part of the ceremony. Diwali prepared his sage in a bowl and got his lighter and feather ready. As he lit the sage and said a prayer, a wind blew in across the room and the flame would not ignite. Puzzled by this effect, Diwali tried a second time to light the sage, and the wind blew even harder and stronger through the open window. Still, the sage would not ignite. This time Diwali decided he would close the window and reopen it after the sage was lit. As he clicked the lighter and aimed it toward the sage, it ignited into a fireball, which caused his fingers to get superficial burns. Diwali dropped the bowl with the sage onto the floor. I ran to the kitchen and got the fire extinguisher from the cabinet under the sink, ran back to the bedroom, and put out the small fire. I got a towel in the bathroom wet with cool water for Diwali to use for his finger burns.

"Are you okay, Diwali?" I asked as I handed him the wet soaked towel.

"I must stop. I have never experienced problems like this before during a cleansing. The evil inside this house and room is not of Indian descent. It does not want me to be here. I cannot perform the cleansing. You will need to find someone else or you will need to do this yourself. I will leave you my supplies. Although, I must warn you that the spirit in this house means harm to whoever tries to make him leave. I cannot say what the outcome might be, but it will not be good."

"Diwali, is there anything else I can do to help you with the burns on your hands? You can put them under some tepid water to soothe them if the cool compress is not helping. I have some over-the-counter pain medicine you may have, too."

"No, ma'am. The evil spirit wishes harm on me and wants me to leave. I need no more treatment. I will take care of it myself. Please protect your family from this house."

I helped Diwali as we picked up the supplies off the floor and he handed them to me. Diwali hurried out the front door, got into his car, and quickly drove off the property. As I stood outside on the edge of the front porch, I noticed the air outside the house was calm. There was no breeze. What just happened here? How could a spirit entity thwart a cleansing with a gust of wind that came out of nowhere through a window that was opened? What made the sage burn so fiercely after the window was closed?

As I held the supplies in one arm, I clenched my fist with the other hand and shook it in the air as I yelled out, "Okay, Jack. You scared off Diwali. If I have to, I'll do this cleansing by myself and you won't stop me! You'll leave this house for good! Do you hear me, Jack?"

When I turned to go back inside, I looked up, and the black mist had moved over my head, just like I remembered from my dream. An image flashed in my mind of a large, evil, devilish beast. I gasped. What did it mean?

CHAPTER THIRTEEN

The house cleansing had not worked. I called Brock and informed him of what had happened with Diwali and the comments he made about the evil in our master bedroom. I told Brock how Diwali saw the black mist over the house like I had seen, and how he got burned from lighting the sage.

"I'm not sure what to make of the whole situation," I said.

"It seems like Jack took control during the cleansing. I hope Diwali will be all right," Brock replied.

"He refused treatment and said he would take care of the burn himself. It stunned him at what happened."

"Jack has proven to be a challenge. Did Diwali give you any other suggestions on getting Jack's spirit out of the house?"

"He left his supplies. I guess I could try the cleansing if I can't find another person who is more familiar with this process than I am."

"Listen, I'm heading out the door with Max right now, and we'll be home in the next twenty minutes."

"King and I will wait for both of you."

Later that evening, the kids had finished homework, dinner, and bath. They went to the living room to play some board games while King sat beside Dex on the area rug. Brock and I sat in the kitchen and talked. Suddenly, we heard King bark non-stop.

"What's up with King?" I asked, puzzled.

"I have no clue. Let's go check it out," said Brock as he stood up.

Just then, Dex ran into the kitchen with King by his side and quickly said, "Mom, Dad, someone is walking in the living room and the lights are acting funny."

"Who's walking in the living room?" I asked.

"I'm not sure, but I know I heard footsteps go towards your bedroom door and stop."

I jumped up and walked with a fast pace into the living room. Brock followed behind me. Londyn, Nox, and Max huddled together on the floor and had stopped playing their games.

"Kids, your brother said he heard something in the living room. Did you hear anything?" I asked, kneeling down as I reached out to comfort them.

"I saw the lights act funny. I thought they might go out," said Londyn with a worried look on her face.

"I heard King bark at the lights, and I heard a board on the floor creak," said Nox as he pointed towards the master bedroom hallway.

"It's Jack," said Max.

"Max, did you see Jack?" I asked.

"Yeah, it was Jack," said Max as he reached his hands straight up and wide.

"I really heard footsteps. I'm not lying Mom and Dad," said Dex.

"We believe you. Everything is okay. Let's get everyone upstairs and ready for bed," I said, trying to remain calm.

Brock helped the kids put away their games. I headed towards our bedroom and turned on the light. There was no flicker, no cigarette odor, and no cool sensation. I checked the bathroom and no messages were on the mirror, only the smudge that would not go away. Everything else checked out okay. I went back to the living room, gathered the kids, and headed upstairs to their rooms.

Brock took one of the classic children's book collections off the shelf in the living room and followed behind us upstairs. He read to the kids and used different voices for the characters as they listened intently. Hopefully, this would get their minds off the intrusion from Jack's spirit.

When the story ended, the kids settled into their beds. Brock and I waited until each one had dozed off to sleep. Then we headed back downstairs to our bedroom.

"I think I should call Father Joseph at church to see if he would do a spiritual cleanse of our home. I don't like our children being frightened by something we can't even see or control," I said, making a note in my phone.

"I'm sure he'll help anyway he can. Right now, we need our rest. The kids have school, and I have work tomorrow. You've got a busy day with Max and King. I Boy Scout promise we'll get this sorted out," said Brock, holding up his three fingers.

I held up my three fingers and said, "I Girl Scout promise to work with you on sorting this out. I don't want to admit it. But I'm getting scared."

Brock leaned over and gave me a hug.

"I'm worried, too. But it's late and we can't do anything tonight. Let's go to bed."

Brock and I crawled under the covers and held each other tight. Brock fell asleep right away in his usual right side position. I stayed awake as I wondered how we would ever get Jack out of our house and our lives for good. Why did we ever move here?

While I lay in bed, my eyes got heavy. My worries about Jack in our house had exhausted me. My mind slowed down as I drifted off into a deep sleep.

All at once, something out there transported my body to another place. It was daylight, and I found myself in a deep hole. There were piles of clay dirt around the top edges of the ground. I saw a figure, a man, who looked down at me, and he had dirt on his gray clothing, hands, and face. The dirt masked his image, and he had a sad expression. I gasped and realized I was inside my dream with the soldier.

Behind this man, I could see darkness in the sky which hovered over him. It came closer to where I was inside this deep hole. Was it going to rain? How would I ever get out of here? The man reached down his arm towards me and gestured for me to grab hold of his hand. I reached out my hand to receive his and instantly paranoia consumed me. Someone else was up there with the man, and my body trembled in fear. There was nowhere to go except up out of this hole and straight towards this darkness. The darkness began to over-power the sky as if night were about to fall. My eyes could no longer see the man that wanted to help me. Where had he gone? Each time I breathed the air, it was hard to fill my lungs. I felt my throat close up. My heart hammered inside my chest, and it ached with great pain. I could no longer breathe. My arms and hands turned bluish-gray. Someone up there in the darkness had a grip on me, and it felt as if I might not make it out of this hole in the ground alive.

I screamed, "God save me." Then, I woke up.

I gasped for air as I sat up in bed. Brock was still lying beside me, sound asleep, and never heard me scream. I tried to reassure myself it was only a dream. Except this time, the dream was worse than the previous one. It felt as if I was ready to die, and I felt helpless. Was my dream a premonition of what might happen? Who was the man that offered me help? What made the darkness want to suffocate me? Had I done something wrong to deserve this kind of nightmare? I believed our house had an evil presence that lived here from the first day I stepped foot onto this property. Now I knew this evil was about to overpower me. Was Jack the evil darkness that came to me in my dream? When I glanced over at the clock on my bedside table, it was three o'clock in the morning.

CHAPTER FOURTEEN

O n Thursday morning, I called St. Elias Catholic Church and spoke with the church receptionist, who connected me with Father Joseph McAfee. I explained that our family was new to the area and the church. We had a spiritual entity in our home that the Shaman attempted to remove during a house cleansing but was unsuccessful.

"I'll set up a time to assess your home today. I can hear the desperation in your voice," reassured Father Joseph.

"Yes, I am desperate. I don't know where to go or what to do. Thank you, Father Joseph, for listening to me." I felt anxious as I took a deep breath in and slowly let it out.

"What's your address?"

"We live at 119 Westview Lane."

"Oh, you're in the old Aster house," said Father Joseph, sounding like he had hesitated at the mention of the address.

"Yes, that's correct. Is there a problem?" I worried he might change his mind.

"Well, let's just say there have been rumors about evil living in that house for a long time." He paused for a moment and said, "I'll be there today at twelve o'clock for the cleansing."

"Thank you, Father Joseph." It relieved me he was coming to the house. Maybe this time the cleansing would work, and Jack would disappear from our lives.

The morning passed quickly and twelve o'clock arrived. Father Joseph would be at the house soon. I would not have a babysitter to watch Max for this cleansing. He stayed in his room for a quiet time with King to keep him company and safely out of the way.

At that exact moment, Father Joseph pulled up in the driveway of our home. I went downstairs to the front door to greet him. He got out of his car and stood there for a minute, just as Diwali had done.

He was of medium height and build, with a bald spot on top of his head that matched his clean-shaven round face and round black glasses. His gray hair on the sides and back of his head were well-trimmed. Father Joseph's white collar stood out against his black shirt, pants, and shoes. His silver cross necklace hung from around his neck to mid-chest. When he moved, the sunlight reflected off the cross in a blinding glare. He held his black Bible in his right hand tightly pressed up against his chest. He walked around the back of the house and returned to the front porch doorway.

"Hi, Father Joseph," I said.

"Mrs. Sterling, have you noticed the black mist hovering over your house?" inquired Father Joseph, looking up towards the roof.

"Please, call me Remi. Yes, I know about the black mist. It's been coming and going since we moved here six months ago. Can you make it go away?" I prayed Father Joseph would say what I needed to hear.

"I will try my best to rid your home of the evil that lies within these walls."

"Please, come inside and look around." I motioned Father Joseph to the front door. He toured the inside of the house, the same as Diwali. When he finished, Father Joseph informed me he could sense an evil aura coming from the master bedroom. I informed him the Shaman had reached the same conclusion.

"Father Joseph, Diwali thought the black mist might be a curse from the spirits of the soldiers buried on this property. He thinks the spirits want to get rid of Jack's spirit from inside the house. He was the owner and builder of this home. The spirits want this house gone, since it's on their burial site. But Jack's spirit doesn't want to leave and wants the house to remain where it is. Our son, Max, has seen Jack in this house. If his spirit doesn't leave, our family may need to move out. So, what can you do to help us?" I asked.

"Oh, I'm afraid I cannot help you, Remi," said Father Joseph.

"What do you mean?"

"This spirit entity has attached itself to your family. I can see you've made some changes to the home. The spirit may not like these changes. This house sat empty for twenty years. Your family has invaded his space. I'm afraid the spirit will become vengeful the longer you live here and the more you change the environment. Your changes to the house are causing the spirit to change, too. The spirit wants to connect with you, Remi, on a more personal level. Have you experienced any other signs of this happening?"

"Yes, Father, I believe Jack's spirit wants me to connect him with his dead wife, Victoria. He wrote Tori on our bathroom mirror. It was a nickname that only he used for his wife. She believed in God, but he didn't. He was an atheist. I believe his spirit is hanging around waiting for her spirit to come back and reunite with him in this house. I've had a connection to the afterlife since childhood, and maybe Jack's spirit expects me to help him. What should I do?"

"I cannot do a spiritual house cleansing. It must come from the owner, whoever it affected the most and is closest to this spirit. That would be you, Remi. You're the one doing all the follow-up on this entity. You're the only one to help rid his presence in this house, but you cannot do it while your family is living here. This house has caused you to be fearful for your family and yourself. First, I would recommend that you wait until you have moved out of the home and it's completely empty of all your items. Next, you must come back to the house alone and perform your spiritual cleanse. This is between you and Jack's spirit. Then, the curse on the home should lift."

"My husband and I are currently working with our realtor on finding our family a new home."

"I wish God's peace with you and your family, my child," said Father Joseph as he did the sign of the cross blessing on my forehead. He placed his hand on my head and said a prayer over me, walked back to his car, and left.

As I watched Father Joseph leave our house, I felt exhausted. Between the move to this house that was haunted, Jack's spirit intrusion, the soldiers in the backyard, the psychic, the Shaman, and the priest, I was at my wits' end. There was no guarantee that any cleansing would ever work on our house. It felt like I was in a losing battle.

"Okay, Jack, you got rid of Father Joseph. Now what?" I yelled, looking around the front hallway. "I won't give up on getting you out of this house. Everyone else might walk away and do nothing, but that won't be the case with me. I'll find a way. You can bet on it!" I fumed, stomping my feet on the wooden floor as I went into the living room toward our bedroom. But after I said all of that confidently, I wondered, what would be my strategy?

CHAPTER FIFTEEN

I decided I could use some professional guidance with my spirit encounters and contacted a psychiatrist for advice. It felt as if Jack's spirit had the upper hand over my life. I needed a grip on reality and not a spiritual entity I couldn't see.

I called Dr. Melicia's office in Cedarville and spoke with the receptionist. Dr. Melicia was at his office in Mumford. There was a cancellation today and his receptionist could setup a visit for me to come in at one o'clock. I took it even though I had no one to watch Max. I called Josie to see if she could babysit for two hours. I needed someone at the house in case I wasn't back when the kids came home from school. Josie agreed and would be at the house by twelve-thirty and would bring her son for a play date with Max. She had errands to run downtown and would stop by after that.

I took Max and King outside to play in the yard until Josie arrived. She beeped her car horn to let me know she was out front in the driveway. Max remembered Josie's son from the playroom at the parent group and was excited to have a friend over. I gave Josie a quick tour of our home, got into the van, and headed down the road to Mumford.

Dr. Melicia's office was directly across from Madame Tallulah's on West Avenue and Court Street. I parked my van on the street outside the brick office building. I entered Dr. Melicia's office at precisely one o'clock and the receptionist greeted me. She motioned for me to take a seat in the waiting room as I prepared to hear my name called.

After a five-minute wait, a staff member escorted me back. Dr. Melicia was an elderly gentleman in his mid-sixties, with thinning gray hair cut close to his head. He wore blue square framed glasses and he dressed impeccably under his unbuttoned white lab coat. He smelled like freshly scented pine needles on a Frasier Fur tree at Christmas. His polished leather shoes glistened in the fluorescent light.

He motioned me to have a seat on the couch in his office. I wasn't sure if I needed to sit or lie down like they had done on the television shows, but ultimately I sat so I wouldn't feel vulnerable.

"Hello, Mrs. Sterling. What brings you here today?" asked Dr. Melicia.

"Please, call me Remi. I came because a spirit haunts our house, and I don't know the best way to get rid of it," I said straight-out.

"Have you actually seen this 'spirit' you are referring to?"

"I haven't seen a physical person, only strange things that occur in our house."

"Oh, what kind of 'strange things' have you seen?"

"Well, where should I begin?" I explained to Dr. Melicia all the instances where Jack had intervened in our lives. First, I started with the flickering lights, the mix of cigarette smell along with a cool sensation in the room, and the sound of footsteps in the house.

Next, I shared with the doctor about our son Max and our dog King.

"One night when I checked on Max in his bedroom, he said Jack gave him some water to drink. How does a spirit do that?"

I informed him that King would bark and growl whenever a spirit entity was nearby.

"He tracks the spirit with his head and lies back down as if nothing happened."

I explained to Dr. Melicia the bathroom incident with the steam on the mirror.

"Someone wrote the word Tori on the bathroom mirror, but no one was around for that to happen. How is that possible?"

"Go on," said Dr. Melicia as he offered me a bottled water from his office mini-fridge to drink. I took a sip as my mouth was dry from talking. I shared the day I saw the original homeowner's deed to our house with Jack and Victoria's names.

"So, my son really saw Jack, and Tori was Jack's wife." Dr. Melicia seemed intrigued by that information.

Continuing on, I explained how each of our family members had experienced a ghost cat on the bed except for Max.

"How can you feel something move on your bed and not see it?"

Dr. Melicia took notes while I continued to talk. I shared the strange smell in our basement that only bothered me and no one else in the family.

"I'm not sure if Jack's spirit causes the rancid smell."

I moved forward on the edge of my seat feeling tense as I recalled the encounters.

"Do you think the two are connected? The smell in the basement and Jack's spirit?" asked Dr. Melicia.

"I believe it's possible."

I shared with Dr. Melicia how Brock's tools fell off his workbench that no one physically touched. In addition, there was a dark figure in the hallway window and black mist that hovered over the house.

"Dr. Melicia, when I was five years old, I had a dream about a soldier in gray clothing sitting near dirt and looking sad. The property we live on looks like my childhood dream. I still have this dream as I have aged. The dream keeps fading and changing over time, and evil darkness looms in the background. This darkness feels as if it wants to take my life away from me," I said, taking a deep breath in and slowly let it out.

"Please, continue."

I explained that my third great-grandfather was a Cherokee Native American who served in the Civil War and wasn't sure if my dream and grandfather connected. "I believe he's trying to communicate with me."

"Have you ever heard of a house cleansing, Dr. Melicia?" I asked.

"I have heard of a house cleansing. How did that turn out for you?"

I went on and explained how the Shaman got burned during the house cleansing, gave up, and left. And how the priest told me to do the house cleansing by myself since he thought the spirit had a hold over me.

"Do you feel overwhelmed by the things you and your family have experienced with this 'spirit' in your home?"

"Yes, I do."

"Do you feel this 'Jack' spirit is real and wants to harm you and your family?"

"Yes, Dr. Melicia. I'm afraid if we don't move out of our house soon, something bad might happen. Our realtor is working on finding our family a new home."

"Do you feel that your third great-grandfather is trying to connect with you as a warning about the house?"

"I believe that Diwali and Father Joseph were right. Evil lives inside the house, and a curse surrounds the outside. I'm not sure what my grandpa has to do with all of this."

"Remi, one alternative you need to do is to coexist with Jack's spirit while you still live in the house, since he doesn't seem to want to leave. Keep in mind that the more you speak of this spirit entity in your home, the more the spirit may respond with more of the things you mentioned in today's visit.

"Let the spirit know that he is in your house, and that you live there now. Set boundaries with the spirit and say the words 'no' and 'stop' if he challenges you. Tell him 'thank you' if he stops the annoying behavior. If your mind continues to be open to the spirit's presence, he will take advantage of this opportunity to stay in your life."

"I never thought of it that way before. But I have told Jack's spirit to leave our family alone, especially our youngest son, Max. It upsets me when I'm talking to something out there that I can't see."

"Remi, have you tried any relaxation techniques to help clear your mind whenever the spirit entity has upset you?"

"I've tried saying my mantra, 'You can do this, Remi, just breathe.' Then, I take a deep breath in and slowly release it."

"That's a splendid start. We offer a class at our office to help with anxiety-related issues. Our receptionist can give you a brochure on your way out. I don't see on your medical form you are taking any medication. Have you had anxiety medication in the past?"

"No, do you think I need something?"

"It's another option you could try to see if it will help calm your nerves and relax your mind. I will give you a prescription today."

"Thank you for listening, Dr. Melicia."

"Here is your prescription. Don't drink alcohol while you are on this medication. Well, our time is up for today. Let's make a follow-up appointment and continue with your spirit concerns. Stop by the front desk and our receptionist will setup your next appointment."

When I left the clinic room, I walked past the receptionist's desk and straight out the door. I decided not to make another appointment. I wasn't sure Dr. Melicia really believed what I had told him, although some of his suggestions differed from what I had already tried at home. Unless you lived in our house, you wouldn't understand all the encounters with Jack's spirit. At least I got all of that off my chest. It was quite cathartic. I would wait on filling the anxiety medicine. I wanted to be alert and on guard the next time Jack showed up.

When I arrived back home, it was two-thirty in the afternoon. The school bus had already dropped the children off at the house. Josie sat at the kitchen table and seemed preoccupied with her thoughts when I walked over to see her. She pointed towards the basement when I asked where the kids had gone. She didn't act like herself. I went downstairs to check on the kids. They were about to finish up their homework and had already helped themselves to a snack. Afterwards, they would head outside to play.

"Mom, we were a little freaked out when Josie let us in the house. We never met her before today. You always taught us to stay away from strangers. Then, you let one into our house," said Dex with unease in his voice. "That's why we stayed in the basement until you got home. Her son came down to play with Max."

"I'm so sorry. I had a big errand to run. Josie is a friend of mine from a parent group I'm attending. You can trust her, if she ever babysits for us again." I gave Dex a big hug.

"Check on her, Mom. Josie seemed a little distracted when we got home from school."

Dex's description of Josie puzzled me. "What do you mean 'distracted'?"

"You know, she seemed worn out and staring off into space. Max and her son must have kept her running all over the house."

"I'll talk with Josie. Keep an eye on each other outside when you go play."

Josie's son was downstairs with Max. I took him back upstairs to the kitchen, and he sat down next to her as I took a seat across from Josie. It concerned me about what Dex had said regarding her demeanor earlier.

"Josie, did everything go okay while I was out?" I asked in a concerned, yet calm tone.

"Well, where should I begin?" Josie had a slight tremor in her voice. "I'm definitely convinced that you have spirit issues in this house." She shifted nervously in her chair.

"Why what happened?"

"Well, Max spilled juice on his shirt, so I took him and my son upstairs to get it changed. While I helped him, I heard someone walking on the staircase. King was in the room with us, so I knew it couldn't be him. The lights in the room began to flicker and King barked. It scared the crap out of me. I looked over at the staircase, but no one was on the steps. I thought it was just my imagination playing tricks on me. Then, Max said the name 'Jack' and pointed towards the door."

"Is that all that happened?"

"No, when we went back downstairs, the kitchen light flickered. What is up with your lights? Anyway, King barked again. When I put the dishes in the dishwasher, it felt like someone slapped my hand and it stung. The plate fell and broke into a thousand pieces. Sorry about that. It scared the living daylights out of me."

"You don't need to worry about the plate. Are you okay?"

"I'm disturbed by the whole thing, but I'll be fine. I'm glad there was still daylight outside when these experiences happened. If it had been nighttime, I would have flipped out. I don't think I'll babysit in your house ever again," she said with absolute certainty. "Everyone at the parent meeting was right about their experiences here. This house is definitely inhabited by a spirit."

Josie was in shock and visibly shaken by what happened at our house today. How could a person who had ever been around Jack's spirit not feel that way?

Josie continued to talk and said, "You're welcome to bring the kids to my house, and I'll watch them there. I don't know how you stand to live here with an active ghost you can't see. He has a flagrant disregard for anyone else who might be in this house. I never would've believed it if I hadn't been here to experience it for myself. I guess all the rumors going around town these past several years were true."

"I'm so sorry, Josie. Thank you for watching the kids for me on such short notice. I'm glad I can share my spirit encounters with you now. Although, I'm sorry you had to have your own. I'll see you at the next parent group meeting, right?"

"Yes, I'll be there," said Josie as she and her son headed out the door to her car without looking back and sped off out of the driveway.

I felt my blood pressure rise and my cheeks flushed red as I yelled, "Okay, Jack. You scared Josie from coming back to the house, and you provoked me until I needed to see a psychiatrist. This is my house and you will no longer live here! I'm tired of your scare tactics. I'm ready to face you, Jack. You and I will meet face-to-face. I will bring you down. Mark my words. I will bring you down!"

CHAPTER SIXTEEN

The February winter sent six inches of snow our way. They canceled Park Grove Elementary and Jamestown University classes. The kids were excited and headed outside to play. They got their sleds and walked to the hill in the backyard. I was glad we had that fence put up right after we moved in to avoid that rocky cliff edge. Dex, Londyn, and Nox each had a sled to lie down on. In sequential birth order, they lined up one-by-one and rode one after the other down the hill. Max and I sat on a smaller round saucer and we glided down the hill together while King barked and chased us. Brock took pictures to capture the moment. I switched places with Brock, so he could be in some pictures with the kids, too. It was a memorable day for our family.

Later, we went inside for a lunch break with hot tomato soup and grilled cheese sandwiches. Everyone couldn't wait to eat. The children's energy was spent as they sled, built a snowman, and threw snowballs at each other. This was how our home should be with happy memories and not haunted ones. Jack had been quiet recently. What was he up to now? Why would his spirit haunt us multiple days in a row and then come to a halt? Life was better when he was non-existent. I had an uneasy feeling Jack would show up again soon. He watched and studied us with every move we made in this house. He would never leave us alone.

After lunch, I stayed inside the house while Brock and the kids continued to play in the snow. King followed close beside me and didn't want to go back outside.

This would be my opportunity, while the house was free from interruption, to do some housecleaning. I went to the basement and got the basket with furniture polish and window cleaner.

I dusted all the rooms. The master bedroom was last. King followed behind me and lay down on the rug. As I cleaned my dresser, I noticed a new smudge on the upper left corner of the mirror. I wondered why I hadn't noticed it before now? It was exactly like the one on the bathroom mirror.

I grabbed the window cleaner and dry cloth. As I wiped the smudge, it went away. I finished cleaning the rest of the room and took my supplies back to the basement. When I went back to the master bedroom, King sat on the rug and growled at the mirror. I knelt down next to him, and his growl stopped.

"What's wrong? It's okay. You're a good boy," I said as I patted King on the head.

When I stood back up, I noticed the smudge returned. I grabbed a tissue from the bathroom and wiped it off, again.

King growled as the smudge slowly reappeared. I could smell stale cigarette smoke and an icy-cold feeling in the room.

"Jack, what are you doing? Are you putting the smudge on the mirror? Are you trying to freak me out? Stop it, Jack! This is not your house. Leave us alone!" I exclaimed, looking around the room and directly at the mirror.

At that moment, King no longer growled and the cigarette odor and coolness left the room. When I reached up to touch the smudge, it remained and wouldn't go away. Neither would the one that lingered on the bathroom mirror. It was the same way with Jack. I couldn't make him go away, either. There wasn't anything more to accomplish, except leave the smudge alone and have Brock look at it later.

After Brock and the kids played all day in the snow, they headed back inside. The kids shed their wet clothes and prepared for a hot bath and pajamas. Afterwards, we ate our dinner and cleaned up the mess.

The kids went to the basement and watched television. Brock and I relaxed in the living room by the lit fireplace as we read and sipped hot tea. I told Brock about the new smudge on my dresser mirror and the similarities it had to the one in the bathroom. I informed him of how the window cleaner wouldn't remove it.

Brock decided he would try. He got up, went to our bedroom, looked at the smudge, and went downstairs to get some type of vinegar water mixture and a newspaper. He cleansed the smudge which worked at first, but after a few minutes it returned. Next, he tried rubbing alcohol. When that didn't work, he tried his shaving cream.

"You're using shaving cream on the mirror?" I asked, surprised by his choice.

"Yes, I read somewhere that this might work when other products fail," said Brock with confidence in the article.

"Go for it, honey. I'm rooting for you." I cheered Brock on while he cleaned.

After several attempts, none of Brock's multiple-product solutions would cut through that smudge. It was a mystery to both of us, and we left it alone for now. We both had a gut feeling that somehow the smudge involved Jack. What other explanation could there be? Brock and I sat back down in the living room and tried to clear our minds about any spirit issues this house had thrown our way. It had become a losing battle. We were feeling numb to our Jack encounters.

After I finished my tea, I headed down to the basement and checked on the children and King. They quietly watched a movie and sipped on their hot chocolate. They looked content and worn out from a fun-filled day. Every day should have been like today, with the sound of playful laughter. I headed back upstairs and cuddled up with Brock on the couch while he read me the sports section of the paper. It wasn't poetry, but his voice was soothing.

I must have dozed off to sleep. And as a result, so did Brock. When we woke back up, it was eight o'clock. We went down to the basement to get the kids. The movie was over, and it was time for the children to head to bed. Max had already fallen asleep in the basement. Dex, Londyn, and Nox ran upstairs and crawled in their beds. They fell fast asleep the minute their heads hit the pillow.

Brock and I headed back to our bedroom and crawled into our bed. We held each other tight and passionately. The love we had shared with our children, our dog, and each other today was an all-consuming love with a bond never to be broken. I never wanted this night to end. We wouldn't allow Jack's intrusion into our lives to spoil the time we had spent together as a family unit. Was Jack envious? Were we the example of the ideal family he had always wanted to have with Victoria but never could?

Brock and I kissed each other good night, and he went to sleep before me. I felt tired and was ready to fall asleep when I felt something near my feet. It stepped on top of the bed and moved up between Brock and me. Ghost cat Sam was back. He hadn't visited lately. What was he up to? I ignored ghost cat and got out of bed and headed to the kitchen. I fixed some hot tea without the added enhancement and watched some television. Once my cup was empty, I felt tired and headed back to the room, crawled into bed, and went straight to sleep.

In the middle of the early morning darkness, a strange sensation startled me awake. This time, it wasn't ghost cat Sam. I smelled stale cigarette smoke and felt an icy chill over my body that made me feel numb. When I turned my head and glanced at the clock, it was three o'clock in the morning. The clock's back light flickered. I glanced over at the doorway and thought I noticed an unknown figure's shape. When I blinked my eyes, the figure vanished. Was I dreaming?

I was too tired to think it might be anything, so I closed my eyes and thought it was just the darkness playing tricks on me. I repositioned myself in bed on my back and lowered my arms down by my side. Suddenly, I felt a heavy weight of pressure lying on top of me. It felt as if someone sucked my breath out from the deepest depth of my lungs and caused them to collapse. A hand reached inside my chest. My lungs were being ripped straight out of my body. I tried to move, but this evil power wouldn't allow me. My mouth opened wide as I forcefully screamed out loud. Why did Brock not wake up to help me? Could he not hear me scream? It felt as if my body were pinned to the bed. What just happened to me? I couldn't move my arms, legs, or head. Was this a dream? If so, I needed to wake up.

I screamed again with all of my strength, "God save me!" Then, I woke up.

Whatever controlled my body had quickly left. I sat up in bed and gasped for air with every breath I took. As I rubbed my neck, it felt like I choked and was about to lose my life. Brock lay beside me sound asleep on his left side snoring, with his good hearing ear exposed. He sensed nothing wrong with me in bed and never heard me scream. How could that be? Everything seemed so real.

Finally, my breathing slowed and I no longer felt the choking sensation. What caused me to feel this way? As I lay back down on the bed, I couldn't go to sleep. My thoughts went straight to Jack. Why did he try to control me? What was his purpose as he choked the breath out of my lungs? Did he want to hurt me and take me down with him to his dark spirit underworld?

There was something different this time about Jack's spirit. He seemed more possessive and aggressive. His demeanor had changed towards me. I could feel myself change along with him. I felt helpless under his spell until I cried out for God to save me. Had he taken offense to those words? Jack gave me a sense of what he could do to me. It was a warning. The next time I might not be so lucky. He meant to inflict harm on me. I wouldn't let Jack control me like that again, but I felt powerless. How could I ever stop him?

CHAPTER SEVENTEEN

My spirit encounter with Jack last night left me exhausted this morning. I informed Brock of the situation that occurred, and we would talk more later this evening.

I followed up with Dr. Melicia about my spirit issue. I called his Cedarville office, and they had an opening at ten o'clock. I contacted Josie and she would watch Max at her house.

I arrived at the doctor's office, and with no waiting, headed on back.

"What brings you in today, Remi?" asked Dr. Melicia.

"Jack's spirit tried to take control of me last night, and I had a hard time breathing," I said, exasperated by this event. I explained how the spirit took my breath away and made me feel like I was going to die. The only way out was saying 'God save me.'

"Did the spirit leave when you said 'God save me'?"

"Yes. What would cause this whole thing to happen?" I asked, as I anxiously awaited the answer.

"What were you doing before going to bed?"

"I watched a psychic medium show and a paranormal show that intrigued me. I wanted to see if I could learn anything about getting Jack's spirit out of the house. Does that have anything to do with what I experienced?"

"Watching a television show about paranormal activities and spirit encounters may have made your mind more receptive to the event you endured."

"I wasn't aware of that. I thought my Christian faith prevented evil spirits from trying to control me. That's why I'm concerned this happened."

"I can see that your faith is important to you. It's clear when you cried out for God to save you and the evil presence left. Do you feel this time your anxiety led to a panic attack when Jack's spirit was near you?"

"I believe this encounter made my anxiety go through the roof. I had all the classic symptoms of a panic attack with a racing heart, breathing problems, and chest pain. Usually, I try to keep it under control with my mantra and breathing. Sometimes I think of a place that makes me happy, like the beach, to refocus my mind away from the problem. These were a few of the recommendations when I had my sleep study. Is there anything different you might recommend?"

"Did you try relaxation techniques from the class or take any anxiety medication I prescribed?"

"No, I decided not to fill the prescription, and I left your office without signing up for your class."

"Remi, I can recommend services and prescribe medication, but I cannot make you do anything you are not willing to do. It is up to you to make that decision. You wouldn't have come here today if you weren't seeking help or guidance."

"You're right. Sometimes as a nurse, I try to solve my health problems instead of allowing the physician to guide me. I'll sign up for your anxiety relaxation class today. I still want to hold off on taking any medication and see how the classes go."

"Great! The class will help you with ways in which to manage your anxiety aside from medication. Stop by the front desk and sign up for the class. Let me know if you see any improvement or not, and we will follow-up from there."

I walked out of the room, up to the front desk, and signed up for the class. They offered one on Saturday in Cedarville, so I wouldn't need to find a babysitter. From now on, I would read a book before bed instead of watching ghost shows.

The last week of February rolled around and what little snow we had melted just as quickly as it had fallen. Dex, Londyn, and Nox turned in their seats on the school bus and waved back at Max and I as we stood on the front porch and watched them leave.

I received a call from Ayesha. She would come by later to take pictures of the house to prepare for the sale. In addition, she wanted us to review some pictures and information on brand new houses in the surrounding suburban neighborhoods. It would excite us to be the first owners of a home and not live in one built on a burial site.

When Ayesha arrived at our house, we went to the kitchen area to talk. I fixed both of us a cup of coffee before we discussed the house. As I sat down at the kitchen table, I asked Ayesha, "If our home is on a possible Civil War burial site with Cherokee soldiers, would the town not want to purchase the land as a historical landmark?"

"That's a good question. I'll follow up with the Cedarville town manager and council. It may need to go all the way to the capital in Richmond for the State of Virginia to purchase the property. They can turn the house into a museum in honor of the fallen soldiers who volunteered from the Cherokee Nation. You can look back one day and say, 'I remember living there' with a sense of pride," said Ayesha with a smile.

"Do you have any interested buyers yet?" I asked, hoping for a positive response.

"Not yet. The sign is at the end of your driveway. I will post the pictures online as soon as I'm done here and have approval from the agency. Don't worry. With all the work you and Brock have done and invested in this house, you will have no problem finding a buyer."

Ayesha walked around the house, taking photos for the real estate website. With each room, she commented on how well the house looked after removal of the wallpaper, fresh application of paint, and the upgrades to the basement bathroom and rec room. Ayesha's camera allowed her to view each photo from different angles of the room and delete any if it wasn't to her liking. She remarked about the backyard not having weeds and the transformation it made to the property. Once they installed the protective fence, it became a significant safety feature which impressed Ayesha. She went over and glanced at the cliff edge past our property line that I had told her about where the trees had fallen and left an opening. It was thick with more trees, brushy weeds, and rocks. She picked up a rock at her feet and threw it down the hillside, but never heard it drop. It had to be a great distance down below not to hear the rock land. She went back to the front of the house and took photos and complimented how formal the porch, stairs, and pillars looked with the trim work done and the ivy taken away.

When she returned to the front door, Ayesha walked inside and upstairs one last time to the hallway area. The photos taken earlier didn't turn out the first time because of shadows from the lighting. She reached over and turned on the hall light. It flickered. As she took pictures, shadows continued to show up in her photo. After several attempts, she decided not to take anymore. She couldn't figure out why this area gave her so much trouble.

Once the photo shoot ended, Ayesha left. I browsed through the pile of new house listings she left us and looked for homes that were in the same school boundary, so the kids wouldn't have to change their school. I wanted our next home to have a level lot, main floor living and sleeping areas, a nice basement, no creaky floors, no repairs, no dead soldiers, no dead pets, and above all else, no dead Jack.

Later that evening, while the kids watched TV, Brock and I relaxed in our bedroom. I took this quiet moment as an opportunity to let him know of my spirit encounter with Jack the night before, my visit with Dr. Melicia, and the relaxation classes. I wondered if he truly believed what I shared with him. How could a dead spirit cause a living person to experience the symptoms I had last night?

"I swear to you, Brock, my symptoms felt real. I thought I was going to die."

"It's a little far-fetched when you think about it. This is the stuff you see in a horror movie—not in real life and not with my wife."

"I screamed for you, and you never heard me."

"Are you sure you screamed? I was lying right beside you. The dog and the kids would have heard you scream, too."

"I could feel myself scream. The air was pushing hard out of my chest, as if I was a balloon being deflated by someone's hands. I swear to you, Brock, every bit was real."

Brock hesitated for a moment and saw how difficult this had been for me. He regretted not hearing me scream and wasn't there when I needed him. He felt as if he had let me down.

He looked me in the eye and softly said, "You know I believe you and that your symptoms are real. If it happens again, shake me awake, and I'll yell at Jack, too." Then he reached out his arms and gave me a bear hug.

I was glad Brock trusted that everything I told him had occurred. My Jack encounters seemed far-fetched, but I experienced these symptoms. It wasn't a dream. I would never lie about something like this.

Brock and I continued to talk and decided we needed a few hours away one night during the week. Our home had made us feel trapped, and we needed to take some time for each other. We wanted to have a date night where we could get out and explore more of Cedarville. It was important for us to connect with the people here and enjoy the different cultures the town offered.

We had attended St. Elias Catholic Church services and Sunday school each week for the past month and made acquaintances with other couples. The church had a youth group babysitting service, so I called the church secretary and she gave me the name and number of Louisa Mack.

I called Louisa and introduced myself. She agreed to come to our home on Friday night around seven o'clock and would watch the children for two hours. She sounded excited for the opportunity, and of course, the babysitting money.

Louisa arrived at our home at exactly seven o'clock. Brock and I greeted her at the front door as she eagerly stepped inside. She was eighteen years old and a senior at Mountain Heights High School. It shocked me when I saw Louisa's hair. It had the same color as one of those pink marshmallow cakes on the shelf at the grocery store. The hairdresser cut her hair short with spiky ends. She was a fashionista, as Londyn would say, with her faded blue jeans, beige UGG boots, black tee shirt, and pink sweater jacket to match her hair. As Louisa pulled off her jacket, she revealed a tattoo on the outer part of her left arm that read 'Oxsana.'

"Louisa, excuse me for noticing, but I see a tattoo on your left outer arm. What does 'Oxsana' mean?" I asked.

"Oh, it's my middle name. It means 'God is with us.' I share the name with my grandmother, who's part Russian," said Louisa.

"Did it hurt when you got the tattoo?"

"It did sting. I pay little attention to it usually, unless someone asks me about it."

At that moment, the children and King ran from the basement to the front hall. I introduced Louisa to the rest of our family, showed her around the house, and gave her a schedule for the children's bedtimes.

"Brock and I have our phones, if you need us. The numbers are on the refrigerator."

"Got it," said Louisa.

"Okay, kids, behave while we are out. Listen to Louisa. If there are any messes, pick up your own, and then help each other," I said.

"Go on your date, Mom and Dad. We'll be fine," said Dex.

We kissed the kids, patted King on the head, and headed out the door. It felt odd leaving our children with a stranger, but we would only be on our date for two hours. What could happen in that amount of time?

Downtown Cedarville was lovely at night. The air outside was chilly, and the sky was clear enough to see a few stars. The smell of grilled steak wafted through the cool, crisp air. Outdoor patio lights glowed in the night as tall aluminum heaters warmed the patrons who braved sitting outside to avoid a long wait indoors. Brock and I had reservations at one restaurant that had a live band. As we entered the front door, the maître d' promptly seated us with our menus.

"Come on, Brock. Let's get up and dance. It's a slow song. Your favorite kind of dance." I teased.

"But we haven't ordered yet," said Brock, looking over the menu.

"The night is young. We'll order after the song," I said, reaching out my hand for his.

Brock gave me a smile and took my hand as we went out onto the dance floor. I put my arms around his neck as he held me close. It had been so long since the last time we had a date and danced. This felt good.

After dinner, we left the restaurant and walked the streets bundled in our winter coats to get ideas for our next date night.

"Brock, let's do this every week. We need this for us," I said, holding his hand in mine.

"You're right. We could use more nights like tonight," said Brock, as he leaned over to kiss me.

I never wanted the night to end. It was perfect. At that moment, my cell phone rang. Louisa was on the other end in a panic and needed us to come home right away.

"Is everything okay with the children?" I asked, saying a quick prayer in my head.

"Yes, they're all in bed. But I'm afraid there's a ghost here and I need you to come home," Louisa said with trembling in her voice.

"Stay on the phone with me. We'll be there in the next twenty minutes. What is that noise on the phone?" I asked as a crackling sound was on the other end and getting louder.

"I don't know what you're talking about. I hear nothing on this end. Please, hurry," pleaded Louisa.

"It's okay. Just stay on the phone with me. Alright?"

"Yes, I won't hang up."

Brock and I got in the car and headed straight home while I kept talking to Louisa, to keep her calm until we arrived.

When we pulled into the driveway, I told Louisa it was okay to hang up her phone. She came down the steps and opened the front door. Brock and I got out of the car and went inside. Louisa was sitting on the steps in the hallway with a look of shock on her face.

"Louisa, are you okay?" I asked, as I placed my arm around her to help keep her calm.

"No, Mrs. Sterling. I'm not okay. This house is scary," said Louisa as her body quivered.

"Let's go sit in the kitchen where you'll be more comfortable, and I'll make you some chamomile tea."

"I'll go upstairs and check on the kids," said Brock.

Brock came back downstairs to the kitchen and reported, "The kids are all asleep, and King is sleeping in Dex's room." Brock took a seat beside me at the table.

"Louisa, start from the beginning, and tell us every detail of what happened tonight."

Louisa began her story. She had made sure the front door locked after Brock and I left to go on our date. She went to the kitchen and fixed a snack for the kids, and everyone headed to the basement rec room along with King.

The children played cards and ate snacks with the television on. Everyone had fun, and King relaxed near the couch. At that exact moment, a clanging noise came from the workbench area, and I heard a strange sound on the floor above the rec room.

Louisa said she told the kids to be quiet and thought she had heard something upstairs. Max had said it was Jack, and Louisa wasn't sure who that might be.

She left the rec room and headed up the basement steps when she heard a noise in the kitchen, like footsteps and what sounded like something falling. She grabbed a broom that was on the hook by the workbench to defend herself and had her cell phone. But she hadn't gotten our numbers off the refrigerator. At that moment, the footsteps in the kitchen stopped as she walked up the steps. When she reached the basement doorway and peeked around the corner, no one was there. She noticed the kitchen light flicker and the cabinet door by the sink was open.

As she stepped closer to the opened cabinet, there was a tin cup with a handle tipped over inside, with something dripping onto the counter. She thought it smelled like gasoline.

She leaned her broom up against the counter, used paper towels to soak up the gasoline spill, and threw them in the trash. She went to the basement and got some rags and a cleaning product. That's when she noticed a glass Mason jar with the lid off perched on the edge of the workbench. It was empty, but she could smell the gasoline.

When she returned to the kitchen, the broom disappeared that she had left leaning against the counter. She looked around for it, but she wasn't able to find it. She washed the tin cup with dish soap and placed it by the kitchen sink.

After that, she took the dirty rags and placed them in a trash bag. When she picked up the trash, she noticed the unlocked dead bolt on the back kitchen door. She didn't know which child opened the door to let King out, while they prepared snacks earlier, and forgot to lock it back when he came inside. She opened the door, went outside, and took the trash to the garbage can.

At that very moment, she heard a thud sound, came back up the steps, the back door was closed, and she couldn't open it. She banged on the door. But the kids were in the basement and couldn't hear her. She banged on the basement window and yelled for the kids to help her, which scared them when they saw her outside. Dex ran up the basement steps, unlocked the back door, and let her safely in the house.

She asked Dex if any of them locked her out of the house and if he had moved the broom, to which he denied any such thing. She looked around the house and made sure everything was in order, but saw nothing out of place or anyone lurking around on the other floors. There were no more footstep sounds in the kitchen after that, and everyone sat down to watch television.

By eight-thirty, she settled everyone in their own bed. She went back to the basement to clean up and heard footsteps above her again. This time she ran up the steps to the kitchen, but no one was there. She checked on the children upstairs, and each one was sound asleep in bed. She felt nervous at this point.

She sat down on the couch in the living room to relax while she waited for us to return home. When she turned on the floor lamp to read a magazine, the light flickered and she heard heavy footsteps going towards the bookcase by the fireplace. She saw one book fall off the shelf and it flew across the room toward the couch. She sat still and held her breath as the sound of footsteps continued towards the master bedroom doorway and the floor board creaked.

Frightened by what occurred, she jumped up off the couch as her heart pounded in her chest and ran to the kitchen. She was so nervous she dropped her phone on the floor. It was at that moment when she called Brock and me about her ordeal.

"I don't think I can ever babysit for you again after the experience I had in this house tonight." These encounters visibly shook Louisa.

"We're so sorry, Louisa," I said as I gave her a hug.

Brock paid Louisa for her time, and I tried to continue consoling her, but she had no more to say and wanted to get out of our house fast. Louisa got up and ran out the front door, got into her car, and sped away.

"Brock, why did you have gasoline in a Mason jar on your workbench?" I asked, puzzled.

"I was emptying the last of the lawn mower gas can to dispose of it. I started working on something else, and obviously, I forgot about it. How did it get upstairs in the tin cup?"

"It had to be Jack. He threw gasoline into the wood-burning stove in the kitchen when he and Victoria lived here. Maybe he was trying to set the kitchen on fire again. This time it was with our kids in the house. He locked Louisa out of the house, probably because he didn't like her tattoo. I think his spirit gets angry at any mention of God. We can't leave the kids alone again in this house, not even with a babysitter. It's time we leave this place for good."

"I agree. Let's get in touch with Ayesha this week and see where we're at on the sale of our home."

Before we headed to bed, Brock and I checked on each of the kids who remained asleep in their rooms. Brock woke up King to let him outside in the backyard for a few minutes and returned inside. He would sleep in our bedroom for the night. The children had no idea what went on with Louisa in the kitchen. I was so grateful God kept our children and Louisa safe.

I walked into the living room and saw the book lying on the floor by the couch. As I picked it up, I noticed it was the children's classic collection book that Brock had read to the kids the other night.

I muttered under my breath, "Why did you throw this book across the room at Louisa, Jack? I'm so mad at you right now. Our family is going to leave this house. You are scaring our kids, our dog, our babysitter, and Brock and me. I hate you, Jack! You are ruining our lives. We're getting out of here. You can have your house. We don't want to live here anymore. Do you hear me? You win. We're moving out!"

CHAPTER EIGHTEEN

B efore long, we rolled into the month of March. The hyacinth in our flower garden was already in bloom and provided a fragrant aroma in the air. Cedarville celebrated spring break early compared to our old school district. Brock was off from his work at the college, and the children from their school. We would enjoy our time off together as a family. We had not planned to go anywhere, since we had things to do to prepare for our move to another home soon. There were a few more updates on Brock's to-do-list. I would pitch in to help wherever I could. The kids enjoyed being home and stayed up late at night to watch television or play board games. During the day, they enjoyed the sunshine, rode bikes, played horseshoe, threw Frisbee, and played ball in the yard.

Ayesha called our house today. She needed to stop by and show us the pictures she would put online for potential buyers. She had informed us a week ago that she was waiting for confirmation from the town or state in handling the property as a historical landmark. There was a lot of bureaucratic red tape with no official proof of a burial site. She didn't want the lack of a decision to hold us up on moving forward with the sale of our home.

At four o'clock, Ayesha pulled up into our driveway. She wouldn't be staying long, as she had another appointment after us.

We stayed outside as we talked about our house.

"I have a question I need to ask both of you. It's about a picture I took of your home recently," said Ayesha.

"Sure, what's your question?" I asked.

"Well, look at this photo and tell me what you think." Ayesha handed Brock and me a copy of the picture. "The outside of your house shows a dark outline of a figure in the upstairs hall window and something dark over the house. I thought a storm was on the horizon. What do you think it could be?"

Brock and I looked at each other, and then we looked at Ayesha. We weren't sure what to think. There was nothing by the upstairs hall window, just a table and lamp on the opposite wall. There was no way I could try to explain that as the reason behind the shadow. Deep down I knew there was only one possibility . . . Jack. It reminded me of the day we were going to the mall, and I could feel someone watching me from that same window.

"Do you have a ghost in the house?" asked Ayesha with a perplexed look.

Thinking about our response, Brock and I stopped ourselves and couldn't say anything. I knew Ayesha was already aware of the haunted rumors when she sold us this home, but she never believed them. This picture was now her proof it was true.

"Yes, we have a ghost, and his name is Jack," I said with a sigh of relief.

"She's right. Jack has been in the house since day one," added Brock. "He hasn't been pleasant to live with either, which is the reason we're trying to move out."

"I guess it's not a rumor about this house, after all. Now, I know it's a fact," replied Ayesha. "A ghost won't affect the sale of your home. Our agency will be upfront with a potential buyer."

Brock gave her a different house photo to use that he took recently, after he landscaped and the paint company completed the trim work. No dark figure was in the window and no black mist hovered over the house. We double-checked the photo just to be on the safe side.

Before Ayesha left, she had followed up on a house I previously told her about in my friend Josie's neighborhood. It was a brand-new, recently built home for sale. Ayesha had looked up the realtor online and contacted him about us viewing the house. There was an opening next Saturday at twelve o'clock. I would need to check with Josie to see if she would watch the kids. We knew it might take longer than expected to sell our current home, and we wouldn't want to miss out on this opportunity.

Ayesha would confirm the walk-through appointment with the realtor. If there were any changes with the date or time from our standpoint, we would let her know. With that, she got in her car and left.

"I'm glad she knows about our spirit situation. I think more people know, but they're not willing to say anything, unless you ask them. If Jack's spirit causes us not to sell this house, what are we going to do?"

"Jack won't stop the sale of our home. It's a grand house and property. We have breathed new life into this place, even if Jack doesn't approve. Ayesha will do her best in finding the right buyer."

I admired Brock's positive outlook, but I wasn't sure I agreed. Jack had done more than give us a scare inside our house. I had a strange feeling that he would prevent me from leaving. Ever since that night when he tried to harm me and take my breath from me, I had an eerie feeling his spirit wanted me to stay in the house with him. He would never stop leaving our family alone, especially me. Would Jack ultimately get what he wanted?

CHAPTER NINETEEN

The photo from Ayesha confirmed what we already knew. Jack was real. Max had seen him. His name was on the original deed, and we heard his footsteps in the house. Now his spirit appeared in a picture of our home. He never liked our family inhabiting his space or the updates that were done. He wanted things left alone and undisturbed as they were when he and Victoria lived here.

Jack did his best to control me. Somehow, I believed he wanted me as a conduit to get to Victoria. She was a Christian and believed, as I did, in God. Her spirit went to heaven when she died. Without Victoria by his side, he was left in his dark spirit underworld alone. He wanted Victoria back.

Later that evening, I had Brock help me move our bed to another wall in the bedroom. I wanted to see if a different position would make Jack leave me alone. It was never clear to me if he actually died in this room. Was his bed against the far wall where we placed our bed since moving here? Did we occupy his space?

Brock and I crawled into bed worn out and went straight to sleep. Every night exhausted me in this house as I tried to manage my life around Jack's spirit. While we were sleeping, something startled me awake at my feet. It was a stepping sensation that moved up between us. Was it ghost cat Sam again? What was going on with this spirit animal? I ignored ghost cat and forced my eyes closed.

While I was in a deep, relaxing sleep, I awoke with a jolt as I heard heavy footsteps which came from the living room. I was lying on my back with my arms by my side. When I opened my eyes, I turned my head toward the clock and the back light flickered. It was three o'clock in the morning. Why was it always three o'clock when I would hear Jack at night?

The bed was now closer to the doorway of our room. I had a better view of one part of the living room. The footstep sounds got heavier and moved closer to our door. Brock still slept and snored, oblivious to what I heard. The footsteps stopped. I looked up and saw a heavily built, tall figure that stood in a silhouette of black, and I could smell stale cigarette smoke. Was I in a dream, or was this real? It had to be Jack.

I didn't say a word and lay in bed perfectly still. I sensed an icy-cold sensation as it slowly crept into the room and a chill ran across my body. As I glanced back at the doorway, the silhouette figure vanished. I took a deep breath in and slowly released it, hoping Jack had left. At that instant, I could feel someone on top of me. It felt heavy. I couldn't move. This spirit entity had me pinned down on the bed. My heart ached. It raced and pounded in my chest, as if it would beat right out of my body. My left arm went numb and my jaw throbbed. It felt like a hand poked through my chest wall and into the cavity, grabbed my heart, and squeezed out the blood. Was this a slow, painful death experience? My breathing became shallow. I choked and couldn't take in a deep breath. In my mind, I thought I would die, and I needed to wake up Brock. My mouth opened wide as I tried to scream but nothing happened. What was going on? I remembered my mantra and thought, "You can do this, Remi, just breathe."

At that very moment, I gasped and was able to take a full deep breath. I forced out a scream as loud as it was possible and cried out, "God save me!"

Immediately, I woke up and felt a release from my body, and sat up in bed. I looked over at Brock. He was still asleep and never heard me scream. Finally, my heart and breathing slowed. The position of the bed in our room had not changed Jack's control over me. I could sense that his aggression was stronger this time than the one before. It felt like I had a heart attack, and my symptoms became extremely unbearable. Was ghost cat Sam warning me about Jack? Was that why he came into our bed to let me know he was close by? What really happened tonight?

Brock had said to wake him up if I had another episode with Jack. I reached over and shook Brock awake. He was still groggy while I told him about the encounter that just occurred. He didn't say anything, but held me close. That's all I needed to keep me calm. As Brock fell back to sleep, my mind raced about what I encountered tonight. I got up and went upstairs to check on the children. They were all asleep in their beds. King slept soundly on the floor in front of Dex's door which remained partially open. No one knew what went on in our master bedroom except me.

I headed back downstairs to the kitchen for some water but stopped first at the hall closet and grabbed the two-step ladder. In the kitchen, I reached for the key in the magnet box behind the refrigerator. When I climbed up the step ladder, I unlocked the cabinet above the sink. This time I got out the vodka and poured myself a glass straight-up. I felt the sting and burn of the liquor.

My body relaxed and my nerves calmed. Alcohol could not be my cure every time I felt scared. These encounters were not my imagination. Tomorrow I would contact my primary care doctor to set up an appointment for a complete assessment of my symptoms and make sure it didn't affect my heart from what I experienced.

The more I thought about tonight, the more my blood pressure rose as I slammed my glass down and fumed, "Okay, Jack, this is turning into a battle now! You can't have me, and you never will. I'm bringing you down. Do you hear me? I'm bringing you down. Nothing will stand between me and getting you out of our lives for good. Got it, Jack?"

CHAPTER TWENTY

After a sleepless night, I felt exhausted once the kids left for school. I sat down at the kitchen table and slowly sipped on a cup of green tea, forgoing my usual coffee fix. I reached for my phone and called Dr. Jessie Baker to see if she had any openings for the day. There was an appointment available in the next thirty minutes. Losing no time, I got Max in the van and headed to the clinic. I quietly fussed under my breath that there wasn't a babysitter available to make this visit a little easier, but if the tables turned and somebody else lived in our house, I wouldn't want to babysit in there either.

Dr. Baker sat down with me after she completed the tests and said, "Everything appears to be fine, Remi. Your heart and lung sounds, blood pressure, pulse, respiration, oxygen saturation levels, and EKG are all good. I'll order some routine labs to confirm my assessment. Right now, you seem healthy. You may have experienced an anxiety attack. You said you're getting ready to move to a new home soon. Stress, raising four children, plus the move to another home may cause physical symptoms that mimic a heart attack."

"I'll be honest with you. There's a reason behind all of this. We have an active spirit living in our house. He's been interfering in our family's life, and especially mine. My symptoms result from his efforts to control me when I'm most vulnerable in my sleep. I was afraid he had done something to my heart. The pain felt so real. I believed I was going to die. I've seen a psychiatrist about this and attended one of his anxiety classes."

"How is that working for you?"

"It's only helpful when I'm actually in the relaxation phase, but once it's over and the spirit shows up again, I'm back at square one."

"Have you tried anxiety medication to help relax your body and mind?"

"The psychiatrist gave me a prescription, but I chose not to fill it. I become more dependent on alcohol to calm my nerves whenever the spirit is around. That's why I haven't gotten the anxiety med filled. This is not like me at all. It started getting worse when we moved into this house."

"I'm aware of the haunted house rumor. I didn't realize it was a fact until now. I'm glad your family is moving to another home soon. I can't force you to take medication for your anxiety. I'll make a note in your chart in case you change your mind. What I recommend is for you to taper your alcohol consumption. It affects your sleep patterns as I'm sure you're already aware of that. Once you're away from the alcohol, we can try the anxiety medication. If you can't stop the alcohol on your own, we'll need to find other options to help you. Does that sound like a plan?"

"Yes, I promise to stop drinking."

I left the clinic with Max in tow and felt relieved I wasn't dying. I drove to the nearest fast-food restaurant, rolled up to the drive-thru, and placed an order to go. Comfort food was the only way to ease my anxiety. I rarely ate fast food, but today was one of those days when I needed it.

Jack had placed a vice-like grip on my heart, lungs, and mind. Somehow my connection since childhood with the afterlife had opened the pandora box for him to enter my very soul as he tried to control me. He wanted me to feel the grief he felt when he mourned the loss of his wife after the fire, and the anguish he felt when his body burned and failed him. The symptoms he experienced through his own pain and suffering were now a part of me.

After we got our order, I pulled into the restaurant parking space. Max and I ate our lunch in the car. Max ate chicken nuggets while I ate a greasy burger, fries, and cola drink.

This was what the doctor should have ordered, I thought.

Afterwards, I drove to the town library and headed inside with Max. This would be a quick visit, so I wouldn't need the receptionist's help. I knew exactly where to go. It was the Self-Transformation section. But first, I grabbed a cup of coffee at the coffee bar and a juice box for Max.

As I thumbed through several books, I looked up spirits and times they appeared. It seemed there was a specific time frame in the early morning hours to be visited by a spirit entity. One book mentioned the hours between three and four o'clock in the morning. While I continued to read, it said this interval was the devil hour or witching hour. Demons and spirit encounters were supposedly active during this period of time.

"That's why Jack bothers me around three o'clock in the morning. It's as if he's following the rules of this book. I wonder if he read it," I mumbled under my breath.

While I was there, I also looked up information on what caused a smudge appearance on a mirror with a spirit in the house. A few books mentioned something about a portal of entrance and exit. Was this how Jack came and went in our home? I wondered if this had been the reason he could write the name Tori on the bathroom mirror. And the reason behind the smudge on the dresser mirror appearing in front of my eyes. Once I satisfied my curiosity with the information I had read, I took Max and left the building to head home.

When we arrived back at the house, I put Max down in his room for a nap and closed the door. King followed me to the master bedroom and lay down on the rug. I lay on the bed while I thought of my carefree place at the beach with sun, sand, and a warm ocean breeze.

My thoughts were interrupted as I wondered what kind of person I would become if a spirit controlled me? Would I wake up one day and turn vicious? Would I harm those I loved and cared for around me? I shuddered at the thought and would not allow Jack the privilege of keeping a tight rein on my life in that way. My family was my priority, and I would protect them to the very end.

When I heard footsteps on the staircase, it broke my concentration. I jumped up out of bed and ran through the living room. King was right behind me. As I got to the stairs, no one was there. I looked up and saw Max's door opened. I knew I'd closed it when I put him down for his nap. I ran up the steps. He was still asleep in bed. I didn't hear anymore footsteps, but I noticed the rocking chair moved back and forth, as it had done on another occasion. King growled as he stood and looked towards the rocking chair. I smelled stale cigarette smoke and felt a chill in the air. I turned on Max's light and it flickered.

I looked towards the empty rocking chair and snapped, "Go away, Jack. You're not welcome here anymore. You're making me think I'm dying when I'm not. This needs to stop! Leave Max alone, too. I told you before, he's not your child. Leave our family alone! Do you hear me, Jack?"

Just then, the rocking chair stopped moving, and King stopped growling. The light no longer flickered, and I reached over to hit the switch and turned it off. The cigarette smell and cold air went away. I couldn't believe his spirit actually listened to me. That's not like him. Jack always preferred to stay in control of any situation he inhabited. What was he up to? At that moment, I was just glad he left us alone. I remained in Max's room for his own safety. I lay down on the rug in front of his bed with King beside me, and we fell asleep together.

Later that evening, I sat down with Brock in our bedroom and informed him of my heart symptoms last night. I wasn't sure how much he remembered since it was early morning, and he was still groggy when I awakened him.

"I thought Jack was going to kill me. My heart hurt and I couldn't breathe. I screamed, and you never heard me. I had to shake you awake. You said nothing, but you held me close."

"I'm sure it frightened you. I don't understand how I can't hear you or feel you moving in bed when this is happening. Are you doing okay?"

"I went and saw Dr. Baker just to be sure I didn't actually have a heart attack. She said all of my tests were fine and suggested I try anxiety medication. I told her I would wait, and that I was doing some relaxation exercises from Dr. Melicia's class. She told me to call if I changed my mind. I also told her I've been drinking more alcohol since my Jack encounters. I have bourbon and vodka hidden in the locked cabinet in the kitchen. I drink to calm my nerves. This isn't who I am."

"I didn't know about your alcohol stash. I'm glad you told me. We can work together on helping you wean off the hard stuff. You're not alone in this. If anxiety medication can help you relax, you should listen to your doctor and try it. The loss of sleep is making you so exhausted. I'm worried about you," said Brock as he reached out to hug me close.

"I'll be okay, now that I know you're going to help me through this. I'm going to call Father Joseph again for some help in dealing with Jack's control over me. I haven't tried the cleansing yet. He suggested I wait until we moved out of the house and it becomes solely Jack's house again. I'll reach out to him tomorrow."

CHAPTER TWENTY-ONE

I knew that the physical symptoms I had experienced in bed the other night were real. I was glad I shared them with Brock. This was not my imagination or hallucination or anxiety. Jack tried to take my soul away from me, along with my heart and the air I breathed. How could a Christian experience an evil physical presence the way Jack's spirit had done to me?

I needed more answers and contacted Father Joseph for divine guidance. He had been at our home, saw the black mist, and sensed the evil presence here. I had set up an appointment to meet with him on Saturday, since he would be there for half a day.

When I arrived at the church, the receptionist escorted me back to his office. We exchanged greetings and he motioned for me to have a seat.

"So, Remi, what brings you here today?" asked Father Joseph.

"Well, Father, recently you learned about our home situation and spirit encounters. Since your last visit, I've had two episodes where Jack's spirit is trying to take control of me."

"Could you tell me more about the spirit's 'control' over you?"

"Yes, of course." I explained to Father Joseph about the two spirit encounters that occurred around three o'clock in the morning. The first encounter involved my breathing.

"It felt as if my lungs were being removed from my body."

The second encounter involved my heart. "It was pounding so hard in my chest I thought someone had reached inside and pulled it out."

"Go on."

"Anyway, Father, my concern is about my faith." I explained to him of my Christian upbringing, baptism, and service to God.

"How does an evil spirit take control over someone of faith?" I informed Father Joseph how I could stop the spirit entity by saying, "God save me."

"It seems as if I'm a different person since we moved to Westview Lane. I'm drinking more alcohol which isn't like me. There have been visits with a psychic, a psychiatrist, my primary care doctor, and now you. Anxiety and panic attacks are a recurring issue. It feels like the spirit in our house is causing me to change into something I don't want to become."

Father Joseph listened intently to my paranormal concerns. He pulled out his Bible and thumbed through the chapters for scripture verses to share with me that referenced evil entities.

"Well, Remi, you've had quite the experience in your home. As a Christian, the Bible tells us to always watch out for the devil. He can take on many forms. It seems you're using the strength which God has given you through the scriptures in fighting this demon. When you cry out for God to save you, as the evil spirit entity tries to command your body, God's Holy Spirit takes over and releases you from this demonic force."

"Will he ever go away, Father Joseph?"

"There will always be evil amongst us, Remi. It's how we as Christians choose to rid this evil from our lives that matters.

Asking for God's help is the right thing to do. Moving out of your home and away from this evil that occupies the dwelling space is the ultimate solution to your spirit encounters. You're never alone, Remi. God is our protector and defender. He will always be with you no matter the circumstances."

"Thank you, Father Joseph. This test of my faith has been daunting, but I will not allow the evil spirit to win. He will not destroy me or our family. Not as long as I have life on this earth."

"God bless you and your family, Remi. God is greater than any evil in this world. Keep your faith strong. It is your greatest defense."

I left the church and got back into my van. As I drove home, I felt encouraged by Father Joseph's words. I wouldn't allow Jack's spirit to rule over my life. It wasn't his to have. I belonged to a greater power than he could ever handle. I was a child of God and that was my stronghold over Jack. I would need to remember that the next time he tried to cause me harm. But when would the next time be, and how much worse would it get?

CHAPTER TWENTY-TWO

T he end of April was upon us, and we were ready to move to our brand new home. When I had spoken to Ayesha about the house for sale in Josie's neighborhood, she went with Brock and me on a tour. She worked closely with the selling agent and helped us with our purchase. Everything moved quickly, with our mortgage loan being approved, and before we knew it, we had the keys to our new house. It was across town in an established neighborhood and closer to Brock's work and the kids' school.

The owner next door to us had sold the empty lot to a contracting business who built the one level living style home with a full basement and worked with a local realtor to put it on the market. The kids were excited, since children at their school lived in the same neighborhood. It thrilled Brock and I at how well all of this came together for our family. We moved at the right time of year, in the springtime, when everything was vibrant with a new beginning ahead for us. Ayesha had some prospective buyers who looked at the home on Westview Lane, and we hoped it would sell soon so we wouldn't have two mortgages for much longer.

On moving day, while the movers helped carry out the last boxes, I packed the rest of the kitchen items and laid out snacks for everybody. The last item that was ready to be packed was the tin cup. At first, I hesitated taking this item with us, but I was drawn to it ever since we moved here. I placed the tin cup back in the metal bread box where I had originally found it and laid it inside the moving box, along with the other kitchen items. I sealed the box, turned to look at the stack I needed to haul to the van, and got started right away.

When I walked back inside the kitchen, the last box I packed was not closed. How did that happen? Maybe the tape wasn't very sticky, I thought. As I prepared to reseal the box with packing tape a second time, I noticed the metal bread box had vanished. Who took the bread box out? I wondered. I'm not sure why I really asked that question. I already knew the answer.

Without hesitation, I grabbed the two-step ladder that leaned against the wall in the hallway and brought it to the kitchen. I unfolded the ladder, climbed up, and looked inside the top shelf of the cabinet. There in the far upper left corner was the metal bread box. I pulled it out and removed the lid. The tin cup was still inside.

"Okay, Jack. You can have your treasured tin cup. I don't want it anymore. I realize now it will only remind me of you, and I don't need that at our new home. Keep it, Jack, along with your precious house," I declared.

I placed the metal bread box with the tin cup back in the cabinet. It was Jack's tin cup, not mine. Finally, I could see that the tin cup was a curse, instead of a blessing all this time, to our home and family.

I got down from the ladder and took the key out of the magnet box behind the refrigerator. I climbed back up the ladder and unlocked the cabinet above the kitchen sink. I poured out the rest of the bourbon and vodka. I wouldn't need mind-numbing alcohol anymore, now that Jack would be out of our home and lives for good. Brock never touched it, but supported me as I weaned myself away from it. What started out as an occasional drink to soothe my nerves from this haunted house turned into more frequent encounters as Jack interfered in my life. This was the reason I didn't want the anxiety medicine. I thought I handled things fine with my own choices. What I failed to realize was how this affected not only my body but my family as well. The drinking would end today.

Brock had arranged for Ryder Varsity to pick up the big items from our home. Everything else that was in smaller boxes would be our responsibility to take in the car and van. Brock took off from work so we could get settled into our new house. The children had today off for the Good Friday holiday. They would play outside and watch Max for me, so the movers could do their job.

We had only been in our home for nine months, but it felt like nine years. When the last box was out, Brock and I looked around to make sure we left nothing behind. The only thing that stayed were the window curtains and rods which didn't fit the windows in our new home.

I went to the master bedroom and left the bowl, sage, lighter, and feather by the window. Everything needed to be out of the house, as Father Joseph suggested, before I could start the house cleansing. The sea salt left in the corners of the bedroom by Diwali was long gone. We packed everything up, and I had no more sea salt as a replacement. It would have to wait until I came back to the house on Monday for the cleansing. Diwali had left me a crystal necklace that I would wear on that day for added protection from Jack.

Over the weekend, our family settled into our new home. They named the streets in our subdivision after trees. Our home was on Oak Drive. Today was one of those days with the sun shining so brightly it gave you an energy boost. It felt good to have a new home in a new neighborhood to start our lives over again in Cedarville. Our kids immediately hooked up with some other children on our street. Their parents brought over homemade meals to get us through the next few days as we got organized. What a godsend this neighborhood was for our family.

Now my good friend Josie would have time to hang out with me. We could be regular exercise buddies while we enjoyed our long walks along the tree-lined sidewalks.

Our new home had a main living level with hardwood floors everywhere except in the bedrooms and basement, which had carpet. The rooms had a cozy feel to them. There would be no squeaky floor boards or ghostly footstep sounds to frighten us.

All four children had rooms up front on the main living level. Brock and I were in the master bedroom towards the rear of the house. It was still close enough to hear the kids if they needed us.

The basement family room was an area where the children watched television and played computer or board games. It was a bigger space than the rec room in the old house. The basement bathroom was charming and didn't resemble an outhouse.

The living room had a gas fireplace to cozy up to on cool evenings. The open kitchen provided easy access for the kids as they grabbed snacks and got back to having fun. King had a padded rug to lie down on in each room of the house with no worry of being interrupted by a spirit or ghost cat while he slept.

Brock and I had a separate study where we read or watched television. There was no stale cigarette odor, flickering lights, or cool sensation to disrupt our lives.

This house worked out perfectly for our family. The backyard was smaller, but it was level for the children as they played outdoor activities. There were no hillsides, large rocks, or cliff edges that hindered their playtime. The subdivision had multiple cul-de-sacs and streets that connected for the kids as they rode bikes safely. Brock and I sat on the front porch and watched the children as they played with their friends. Life was good again. We were free from spirit encounters.

The weekend went by quickly. Then Monday came, the day I had been dreading. It was time for the house cleansing at our former residence. Brock took the day off to watch Max for me. Dex, Londyn, and Nox were at school. King followed me outside to the van to see me off. As soon as I opened the van door, King jumped inside.

"King, you need to stay here with Dad and Max. Come on and get out of the van," I said as I pulled on King's collar. King sat in the front passenger seat as he pulled back and resisted my futile attempts to remove him from the van. He was adamant about staying, no matter what I tried to say or do to make him leave. At that moment, Brock popped his head out the front door.

"Is King with you?"

"Yes, he jumped in the van, and he won't leave. I guess I'll take him along for the ride."

Brock walked over to the van and tried to get King to move, but he wouldn't budge. "Remi, are you sure you want to do this? I don't like that you're doing this alone. Max and I could pile into the van and go with you."

"No, I'll be fine. This is something I need to do alone—it's between Jack and me. Father Joseph said once everything was out of the house, I needed to be the one to do the cleansing and get rid of Jack's spirit. It's a cleansing for me, too. I Girl Scout promise I'll be back within the hour," I said, holding up three fingers.

Brock gave me a kiss and a hug. The smell of his spice cologne gave me a sense of comfort. With King in tow, we left the house and headed to Westview Lane. I prayed it would be the last time I would ever have to go down that road and into that house ever again. As I drove, I remembered when we first arrived in Cedarville. There were many things that happened to our family and to other people who entered into our home. I was glad it was behind us and our family had safely moved away and moved on with our lives.

Finally, I reached my destination. I saw the black mist as it hovered over the outside of the house while I drove up the gravel dirt road.

"I can tell already this won't be good," I remarked aloud as King barked.

I pulled into the horseshoe driveway and parked. King got out of the van with me. I called King and motioned for him to get back inside the van to wait for me until the house cleansing ended. He wouldn't go. I pulled on his collar and still he wouldn't budge.

"King, you're so stubborn today. Why won't you listen?" I asked, exhausted from the effort.

"Okay, boy, come in the house with me."

King and I entered through the front door. It seemed strange that no one else was home, and no furniture was there. It was eerily quiet. I felt anxious about this whole situation. My stomach was queasy, and I wanted to run back out the front door and forget about this entire process. But I knew if I didn't go through with this cleansing, Jack would not return to the dark spirit underworld where he belonged, and I wouldn't feel completely free in my mind from the things he had done to me even though our family had moved on. I turned on the hall light switch and it flickered. There was an icy-cold feeling in the air. King barked.

"It's okay, King. Calm down," I said as I patted his head.

"I know you're here, Jack. The smell of your stale cigarette odor is right where I'm standing. I'm keeping my promise. Do you remember what I said before? I'm taking you down with a fight to the bitter end. Victoria no longer lives here, and died in the house fire you started. She believed in God and went to heaven. You cannot be united with her. I am not your conduit. You never believed in God and did this to yourself. We all make choices in life, Jack. Your choice separated you from Victoria forever. You'll never see her again. Go back to your dark spirit underworld, where you belong. Do you hear me?"

"King, stay at the front door," I said as he obeyed and sat down without hesitation. "Wow, you finally listened to me."

When I walked back towards the master bedroom, my legs felt heavy as I dragged along with each step. The cleansing items that Diwali had given to me were on the floor by the window where I had left them before we moved out. I had brought some sea salt from the house and placed it in the corners of the master bedroom.

I knelt down and picked up the bowl with the sage and the feather in my left hand and the lighter in my right hand.

While I picked up the supplies, the crystal necklace I wore moved off center from around my neck and got tangled in my hair. My hands were full while I held the cleansing supplies. I adjusted the necklace position and undid the tangle. At that moment, the clasp broke on the crystal necklace. It fell towards the floor as I fumbled to catch it. When it landed, I knelt down to pick up the necklace and placed it in the pocket of my sweater jacket.

When I stood back up, I saw something out of the corner of my eye and turned around. I gasped. Immediately, his left hand gripped my neck and applied pressure, causing me to choke. I felt paralyzed.

There he stood in all his deathly glory . . . Jack. He was big and tall, just like Max had described him to me. The silhouette I had seen in the doorway that night while lying in bed was this grotesque figure that stood in front of me now . . . Jack. He wore all black from head to toe and a black mist surrounded him, just like the black mist that hovered over the outside of the house.

I stared at Jack's face. It was gray and wrinkled like an apple that had rotted, or it may have resulted from his burns in the house explosion. Who really knew? His cold, powerful hand squeezed my neck harder. He smelled like rotting flesh. The stench of death overwhelmed me. It was the same dead animal odor that I smelled in the basement drain that day. The smell only I recognized where his energy was at its highest, near the water and sewer.

I stared into Jack's piercing red eyes, which resembled a devil's pitchfork. With each breath I took, I felt Jack's hand as it became stronger and started to cut off more of my air supply. I wrestled with Jack as I moved my body backwards to get closer to the window and out of his grip. I jabbed my left elbow back and broke the windowpane for his evil spirit to escape as part of the cleansing. The broken glass was jagged and cut through my thin sweater and shirt into the back of my left upper arm. My flesh tore as I pulled my arm out. Blood gushed from the opened wound, ran towards the tips of my fingers, and dripped onto the floor.

I felt weak. The sage bowl and feather had dropped out of my left hand when Jack grabbed my neck, and now they laid on the blood-stained floor. I was light-headed and would pass out soon.

"You can do this, Remi, just breathe," I thought. I had to stay awake. I couldn't let Jack take my life away from me. I wouldn't let him win.

Somehow, I held on to the lighter with my right hand. With the strength I had left, I clicked the lighter, but it didn't ignite. The shattered glass window allowed the wind to blow across the room which hindered the flame. I clicked the lighter a second time and still nothing. This time the wind blew even harder.

Oh no, this was what happened to Diwali, I thought. I clicked the lighter a third time, and the flame slowly ignited. I knew my time would run out any minute. I quickly aimed the lighter towards the sage, but it had fallen out of the bowl when I dropped it during my struggle with Jack. It landed near the curtain by the broken windowpane.

"Please God, don't let the flame blow out," I silently prayed.

With all of my might, I edged myself closer to the window and the sage on the floor. I stretched my arm down as far as I could reach to ignite it. I could smell the sage burn and noticed the curtain caught on fire. At that moment, I dropped the lighter and both of my arms went up to get Jack's hands off my neck. My arms and chest burned. Now I knew I would die in this house.

Suddenly, I heard a strange sound. Jack tried to speak to me over and over.

"I . . . want . . . Tori." His voice had a slow, deep, garbled sound like a record that played backwards. Was I hallucinating from lack of oxygen to my brain? Had Jack really said those words?

At that moment, all I said as I tried to gasp for more air was, "God . . . save . . . me!"

Those words made Jack become even angrier. This time he wouldn't let me go as he had in the past. Maybe the fire in the room reminded him of where he should be in his dark spirit underworld. Immediately, Jack choked me even harder around my neck. Now, he was using both of his icy-cold, dead hands to squeeze what brief life I had left inside of me.

Just then, in my panic, I saw something else behind Jack. Another figure had emerged, but my blood and oxygen supply that Jack cut off caused my vision to blur. I wasn't able to see who or what it might be. The figure looked like a woman and stepped closer to Jack. I barely saw a face.

Who was this person? I thought.

I would not have enough air left to breathe and find out. My voice could no longer make a sound. I heard King bark. It was my time to die. My last breath left my body. Then I blacked out.

CHAPTER TWENTY-THREE

S tartled awake by what seemed like a long nightmare, I shivered in my bed not knowing what it meant. I clenched my jaw tight and opened my eyes wide as I held my covers close to my body and looked around at my surroundings.

Where was I?

The starch white barren walls, faded blue blanket on the bed, sunken mattress, and the nauseating smell of rubbing alcohol which lingered in the air made me realize I was in a hospital room. The vertical blinds on the window were opened, which allowed the sun's blinding glare to slap me in the face as I held up my hand for a shield.

Wait a minute, why do I have bandages on my arms, neck, and chest? How had I ended up in a hospital bed? I knew this was the Intensive Care Unit. I recognized one nurse outside the glass break-away door as she sat at the desk. Why would I be in ICU? I was healthy, not sick. What day was it? How long had I been in the hospital?

While I got my bearings to my room, I was distracted by the noisy beeps of the surrounding machines. The intravenous pump chirped loudly as the fluid bag had run out. Blood backed up in the tubing connected to my left hand. There was oxygen on the wall behind my bed with a humidifier bottle attached to the flowmeter that made a sound like boiling water on a hot stove. I had electrodes attached to my body for the heart monitor, which beeped off tempo with the I.V. pump.

"Someone please, stop this noise," I said to no one in the room.

Whoa, why was it hard to talk? I wondered. At that moment, I had the urge to pee and wanted to get up out of bed but realized I had a foley catheter. Why?

"Get this thing out of me, it hurts," I exclaimed, as my voice could barely echo off the walls. What happened to me? Why did I have all these tubes and bandages? How did I get here?

As I reached for the call bell, I looked up and noticed there were doctors and nurses who had congregated outside my glass door. They talked amongst each other and watched me intently.

As I lay in bed, I thought back and retraced my steps from my most recent memory. I remembered I went to the old house, King stayed at the door, I walked to the master bedroom and then Jack revealed himself to me. After that, I couldn't remember anymore. There were only bits and pieces of memory recall with gaps in between. I needed more information to put the puzzle together.

Suddenly, one of the healthcare workers slid open the glass door and interrupted my thought process. She swiftly walked over to my bedside. As this person came closer to me, I recognized her face. "Remi, thank God you're awake. You gave us quite a scare. Let me get your husband. He's been waiting to see you," said Dr. Baker as she turned and motioned for someone to come into the room.

Just then Brock walked in. He gave me an enormous hug as his eyes welled up with tears.

"Don't cry, Brock. I'm okay. Everything's fine. My throat feels sore. I'm hoarse. What's going on? Who brought me here?"

"The ambulance brought you to the emergency room. We almost lost you, Remi."

"What? An ambulance? How can that be?"

"The house caught on fire and burned to the ground."

"What? Oh, no! What happened?"

"A neighbor down the road saw the smoke and called 911. When the emergency crew arrived, you were outside the house laying in the front yard. King was lying beside you."

"King, is he okay?"

Brock paused as tears flowed from his eyes and down onto his face. "King saved your life, Remi. He was a genuine hero. He gave his life to save yours."

"What? No, no, no! He was at the front door. I told him to stay," I said as tears streamed down my face.

"He must have known you were in distress and ran to the bedroom to drag you outside from the fire. You must have left the front door cracked open as part of your cleansing ceremony. He died from smoke inhalation after he rescued you. The medics tried to revive him, but it was too late. We had to bury him while you were in the hospital in a coma."

"I don't remember leaving the front door open. I was going to open the window in the bedroom for the cleansing ceremony."

"It doesn't matter, Remi. King got you out of the burning house."

"How long was I in a coma?"

"You were in a coma for three days. The doctors had to put you on a ventilator so your lungs could heal from all the smoke you inhaled and the burns you got on your neck, chest, and arms. The doctor said you had bruising to your larynx and trachea, too. They took you off the ventilator twenty-four hours ago. We've been waiting for you to wake up on your own."

I was literally in shock. I couldn't believe our beloved King was no longer with us, and he had saved my life. He followed me everywhere I went. What would I do without him by my side and his protective watch over the kids? He was my baby, too. "It's not fair, Brock. Why did this have to happen?"

"I don't know, Remi. If King hadn't been in the house, you might be dead right now, instead of in the hospital recovering," cried Brock, wiping away tears and reaching out to hold me closer.

"Where did you bury King?"

"We buried him on the land where the house burned down. The State of Virginia has purchased the property with plans to build a War Memorial."

"Are the kids okay?"

"Yes, they're fine. They miss King, but they know he took care of you and that makes them happy."

"What about Jack? I saw him, Brock. That's why my throat feels this way. Jack tried to choke and kill me," I said as tears flowed down my cheeks.

Brock reached up and wiped away my tears. "Hopefully, Jack burned along with the house and its memories. I'm so sorry, Remi. Jack's spirit obsessed over you. I didn't realize how real all of this was until I almost lost you."

"Wait, Brock. I think I remember something else about that day. When Jack was choking me, I thought I saw the figure of a woman standing behind him. Things were a little blurry, but I believe it may have been Victoria. Who else could it have been? She had to have been the one in the room right before I blacked out. I think I heard Jack call out her name. When you said the front door must have been open, I had left King sitting there. I didn't want him to go outside without me. The glass storm door was closed. Do you think Victoria helped release Jack's grip on me and opened the door so King could drag me out of the house?"

"I don't have the answer to that question. I'm willing to believe anything after what our family's been through."

"I want to go home, Brock. Please, get me out of here," I pleaded as I clung to him.

Dr. Baker released me from the hospital three days later. They would remove the sutures to the gash on the back of my left upper arm next week on my follow-up visit. I would always have a scar to remind me of that fateful day with Jack.

The burns on my neck, chest, and arms continued to heal and would leave a scar. I would need to keep a bandage on my burn areas, have it changed daily, and closely monitored for any signs of infection while I recuperated at home. Dr. Baker said I must have had my arms up when I was burned, which helped protect my face from the fire. Plus, King dragged me out of the burning house before I received severe burns to other areas of my body. Some hair on my head had gotten singed, which would need to be cut off. I guess I could use a new hairdo. Home Healthcare would visit me for a week at the house for follow-up care.

As I prepared to leave the hospital, the nurse brought in my discharge papers and a small manila envelope. She told me my clothes had to be cut off in the emergency room because of my burn areas, so they threw them away. But they got my jewelry and saved it in the envelope. Inside, I found my wedding band and engagement ring. My fingers had some swelling since my arms burned, so I placed the rings back in the envelope and would put them in the jewelry box when I got home. I looked back inside and expected the broken crystal necklace to be in there. Instead, I found a gold cross necklace. I told the nurse it must have been a mistake, as I had never seen this necklace before.

"No, Mrs. Sterling, this is the necklace we found in your sweater pocket the day you arrived in the emergency room," she said.

"Oh, okay. Well, thank you," I said with a puzzled look.

I examined the cross necklace closely. As I turned it over, I noticed three initials, VMA, engraved on the back.

"Who is VMA?" I wondered. Then, I gasped and said aloud, "Victoria Aster."

I had the nurse put Victoria's necklace on me and showed it to Brock when he came to pick me up from the hospital. It shocked him to see the necklace and Victoria's initials.

I received my discharge papers, and Brock drove me home. We wanted to put this entire ordeal behind us. Josie had watched the kids at our house until Brock and I arrived. I still felt weak, but grateful to be back at the house with our family.

When I entered the front door, Dex, Londyn, Nox, and Max ran towards me and yelled, "Mommy's home!" and gave me a big group hug. They had surprised me and fixed pancakes for dinner with Josie's help.

Josie gave me a gentle hug and said, "I'm glad you're home, too." Then she headed back to her own place and said she would check on me later.

Our family sat down at the table and we ate our pancakes, laughed, and looked at pictures of King while we shared our memories of all the silly things he had done. He would always be in our hearts forever. I glanced down to where we kept King's bowls and noticed they were still on the kitchen floor full of food and water. None of us had the heart to empty them, yet. I would miss that big ole dog.

The months had rolled by quickly. My wounds had healed, but the scars remained. During the summer months, the kids grew another inch or two. It was only a matter of time before they would be taller than me. Our family spent time at the lake, rented a cabin, took a boat ride, and cooked s'mores over a firepit. We rode bikes and hiked a short loop trail along the wooded hillside. The fresh air and sunshine relaxed me. The kids swung on a rope and jumped into the lake while Brock and I cheered them on.

Before we knew it August arrived, and school started again. I wasn't sure things would ever feel normal after everything that had happened with Jack.

As I sat outside on the front porch in the rocking chair, I soaked up the warmth from the sunshine. The kids had started back to school, and they had promoted Brock to department head in landscape architecture at the university. Max got into daycare two days per week part time which gave me some free time. Some days Josie and I would take a walk in the neighborhood or go to town to shop or eat out for lunch. I treasured our friendship.

Today, I was at the house by myself. I had not gone back to my work as a part-time nurse yet. I still needed time to heal physically and emotionally and wanted to be here for the kids when they came home from school.

It was at that moment I got into the van and went for a drive to Blue Stone Funeral Home. It was located downtown near St. Elias Catholic Church. I spoke with Mr. Oakland, who was the owner.

"Hi, Mr. Oakland, my name is Remi Sterling. We've met once before. I was wondering if you could help me find a grave marker on a person."

"Of course, Mrs. Sterling, who might you be looking for?"

"I'm looking for Victoria Aster's burial site."

"Oh Mrs. Aster, she was a fine woman and very generous in her giving to this community. I didn't know her personally, but I know of her from others who shared about her kindness, love of people, and her faith. I'm sorry for my rambling. Let me look up that information for you." Mr. Oakland quickly got on his computer and looked at the location of Victoria Aster's grave marker. "Regarding your question, Mrs. Aster's remains are in Blue Stone Memorial Garden. It's off the main highway. You can't miss it. Just look for the sign. She's in the columbarium at the end of the cemetery lot. Go inside the building. It will be on the left wall, the second row down from the top, and the third marker over."

"Thank you, Mr. Oakland."

I headed back to the van and drove down Main Street. There was a sign up ahead that read Bluestone Memorial Garden. It had a formal entryway with a stone wall and columns. While I drove through the cemetery grounds, the lush green, well-manicured lawn impressed me. It looked like a golf course. No tombstones were present only flat markers which made it easier for upkeep on the lawn. Families placed flowers in vases that sat on top of the markers.

There was a light brown brick building at the end of the cemetery road. I parked the van in the space and went inside the double glass doors to the columbarium. There were grave markers on all three sides of the wall. I walked over to the left side and looked for the second row down from the top and the third marker across. There it was. The marker I was looking for. It read:

Victoria Marie Aster

Born 1919

Died 1998

Child of God

Beloved wife of Jack

Friend to all

I raised my hand up towards the marker and said a quiet prayer for Victoria and what she had done for me that horrific day.

"Victoria, thank you for helping save me from Jack in the house fire and helping King get me out of the house safely. I remember seeing a woman's figure and a face briefly, before I blacked out. It was blurry, but now I know it was you. I don't know what happened to Jack and whether or not he saw you. Maybe he went back to his dark spirit underworld. Please know that I am forever grateful that God sent you as my guardian angel to help me. I will see you again someday. God bless you, Victoria."

After my prayer, I lowered my arm and turned around to leave. Just then, I saw someone who watched me intently in the far back corner of the room. She was slightly heavyset and had on a floral dress with high heeled black-laced ankle boots. Her brown hair had a touch of gray at the temples and pulled back into a bun. The woman stood there as she delicately held a Siamese cat and stroked its fur. I knew exactly who this person was. The blurred figure and face were now plain to see and forever etched in my mind.

"Victoria and Sam, it's nice to meet you," I said, staring in amazement. "Victoria, Sam would visit Brock and I in our bed at night walking in between us. He must have done the same in your bed, too." Victoria smiled back at me. "Each time I cried out for God to save me from Jack, he sent you as my guardian angel to distract Jack away from me." Victoria nodded her head in agreement. I pulled the cross necklace from around my neck and said, "You left this cross necklace in my sweater pocket. These are your initials on the back." Victoria smiled and nodded her head downward. "I will always wear this necklace as a reminder of your kindness and faithfulness. Thank you, Victoria and Sam. Keep watching over our family." Victoria smiled and waved. Then she held Sam close to her as she walked towards the back of the columbarium room and faded from view. "That is so cool," I remarked aloud.

I left the columbarium and was shocked to have seen Victoria and Sam. I felt comforted that I wasn't going crazy with some of the spirit encounters at the house. They were real. I got in the van and drove out of the cemetery. I needed to make a quick stop at the farmer's market downtown before I headed to my next destination.

After I finished my errand, I headed straight to Westview Lane. When I arrived on the property, it was the first time I had been back since the accident. It seemed strange that the house no longer sat on the hill. The department responsible for the preservation of the property had already done work to fence off the graveyard site. It included the area where the house had burned down and everything behind it towards the hillside. There was a sign that said they would erect a new building on a different section of the property away from the gravesite and it would be a museum for the Cherokee Veterans. Excavation on the property would continue.

I parked the van and got out. Outside the fenced area, there was a small grave where they buried King. We placed a flat marker with an etched picture of him, so our family could come by and visit. Also, the land preservation department had acknowledged that King helped find the location of the hand grenade on the property which proved it was from the Civil War Era. Now they recognized him as an official contributor to the museum.

I placed a single red rose on King's grave that I had picked up at the farmer's market. I blew him a kiss as I touched his gravestone marker and said, "I love you, King. Thank you for saving my life. I'll see you again one day."

As I stood up to go back to the van, something caught the corner of my eye. In the far distance of the graveyard, there stood a man. He had olive skin that was no longer covered in dirt, and he wore a gray Confederate uniform. I felt no fear as I looked at him. His image was no longer blurred.

The soldier came to the edge of the fence and stopped. I walked closer to the fence to see him. I saw his name tag as clear as day. It read J. Awahili. It was my third great-grandfather.

"Grandpa Jake!" I said, elated. "It's nice to see you standing in front of me. You were the soldier in my dream, when I was a little girl. My dream kept fading and getting darker as I got older. I couldn't see you clearly anymore." Grandpa Jake smiled. "It was you who led King to the site in our backyard to dig up the grenade. You wanted to help prove there was a burial site on the property. It was your grenade, wasn't it?" Grandpa Jake nodded his head in agreement.

"The tin cup that I found in our kitchen cabinet was yours, wasn't it?" Grandpa Jake smiled. "The initials JA on the bottom of the cup stood for your name, Jake Awahili, and not Jack Aster. I had it wrong. All this time, you were trying to communicate with me. You were waiting for me to come to this house. Your spirit wanted me here to help set you and your fellow soldiers free. I'm so proud of you, Grandpa Jake."

Grandpa Jake put his right hand up to his chest and over his heart and smiled at me. Simultaneously, he turned back towards his left and held out his hand. He motioned someone to come forward. Up over the hill, I could see something in the distance as it ran so fast.

"King!" I yelled.

Grandpa Jake held out his hand and motioned for King to stop. He sat down beside him. Then he patted King's head, just as I had always done.

"I love you, King. You're a good boy," I said.

I looked over at Grandpa Jake and said, "Take care of each other till we meet again."

At that moment, I noticed other men in gray uniforms at a distance, and they smiled and waved in my direction. I acknowledged them with a salute. I watched the other soldiers, Grandpa Jake, and King as they walked away towards the wooded hillside and faded from view.

"How do they do that?" I remarked aloud.

I was glad I saw King and knew that he would never be alone. He had a family member in Grandpa Jake who would take care of him on the other side.

CHAPTER TWENTY-FOUR

M ore than a year later, our family enjoyed the new house on Oak Drive. Max hadn't mentioned Jack's name or seen him after we moved out of Westview Lane. I hadn't asked him about it either.

We got another German Shepherd and named him Jake, after Grandpa. The kids loved to play with the puppy. He looked exactly like our beloved King.

My childhood dream had gone away, but I still had an uneasy feeling in the back of my mind. I wasn't sure how that could be when the worst of my fears about Jack subsided. I supposed it could have been post-traumatic stress disorder. The entire family had experienced it. Heaven knows I had my fair share of it in our former house. My scars were a constant reminder.

The smudge on the upper left side of my dresser mirror faded away. After we moved into our new home, the smudge had disappeared on its own with no special cleansers used and never returned. Could it have been Jack's portal, as the book I read at the library had suggested? I was glad it was no longer a visible reminder that looked back at me every day.

September brought the opening of the Cherokee Veterans Museum, and our family had a special invitation. Everyone piled into the van, and we headed to the museum. We wanted to be there to support my third great-grandfather, Jake Awahili, and his service to our country. He and his fellow soldiers were now free from the house that Jack had built on top of the graveyard so many years ago.

We were excited to see some of our community friends at the grand opening. People from all walks of life would learn about the brave Cherokees from North Carolina who volunteered in the Civil War and the five wounded Cherokee soldiers who returned and made Virginia their home. They wore Confederate soldier uniforms even though they supported the Union side to abolish slavery.

As our family walked through the museum, we learned that those five Cherokee soldiers who served in the Civil War were on this property buried together. As a memorial, the families had these men buried near each other on the same piece of land to honor their camaraderie and service.

When they excavated the land after the house burned down, the exhumed artifacts were placed on display in the museum. They found war items that the soldiers families buried with them. Scattered on the property were bone fragments, pieces of decayed uniform, parts of a breastplate, Civil War belt buckles, rifles, dog tags, canteens, swords, pocket watches, toolkits, and even a Bible with a musket ball stuck inside. The opened Bible on display showed the Book of Psalm 23, where the bullet had stopped.

We saw the rusty hand grenade in a glass case that King had dug up, along with his picture that Brock took of him in the backyard. King was so proud of himself that day. They awarded him a medal from the State of Virginia for his bravery since he found the grenade and saved my life that fateful day. I cried as our family accepted it. The museum would give King's medal its own display case.

"Isn't it amazing all the items buried with these soldiers?" I said, looking around at the exhibit.

"Yes, it is. This has turned out to be a beautiful tribute for the men who served and for King. Excuse me while I catch up with the kids. It looks like their motioning me for some money," said Brock as he hugged me and walked over to the refreshment area.

I headed off in the opposite direction to follow the tour guide, Ms. Kamama. She floated around the museum like a butterfly. She delicately moved her arms left and then right, similar to a showcase hostess who had a prize to present. As Kamama led the people through the museum, she gave detailed information about the items that were on display. Each one had the name, date, and use in the war. There were war pictures of Cherokee soldiers who volunteered during that era. I glanced at the photos and found Grandpa Jake in a few of them.

If only these visitors knew what happened for these artifacts to be found. This was what our family helped to unearth and what Grandpa Jake tried to share with me in my childhood dream.

Now it had all made sense, I thought.

I wandered ahead of the tour group. As I turned the corner, I noticed an item on display in the middle of the floor. The museum enclosed it in a clear glass dome on a pedestal. It had a light that beamed down on it. The tour guide showed up at the same time with a group of people who followed behind and moved around me.

She stopped at the object and said, "Ladies and gentleman, this object under the glass dome is part of the war items. The excavators found this particular item after a fire burned down the house that was located here. This item hid in a metal box and they found it in the bottom drawer of the stove. It was a drinking cup used by one soldier buried on this property. The initials JA are faintly on the bottom of the cup and stand for Jake Awahili. The original owner of this property had left behind a letter upon his death with background information on the tin cup and the tin cup owner's name. The preservation society received a letter when they purchased the property and it is currently on display in the museum. We're still gathering data on the person this cup belonged to for official recognition of his service to our country. We wanted to keep it separate from the other items until we have more information. Now, if you will follow me to the next area . . . "

I gasped when I heard Ms. Kamama say Grandpa Jake's name. I walked over to the tin cup in the display case. I bent down for a closer look. I remembered the first day I took it from the far left upper corner of the kitchen cabinet hidden in the metal bread box and placed it by our sink. The letter she spoke of was in a separate display case near the tin cup. I walked over to have a look. The letter was written and signed by Jack Aster with detailed information about the tin cup he had found on his property.

In the letter, Jack Aster had written that in 1940 he built the house at 119 Westview Lane and found the tin cup buried at the house foundation site.

The letter continued and said Jack searched for information about who might have been the cup's owner with the initials JA engraved on the bottom. He followed up with the courthouse to see if there was any documentation of a gravesite on his property. They found none. He went to the town library where his research led him to a Civil War book that included a picture of a tin cup used by Civil War soldiers. He looked in the glossary index under 'Virginia' and found information on Cherokee Native Americans who volunteered in the war.

The historical letter said that Jack checked with the nearest Cherokee Historical Association in North Carolina. A volunteer registry confirmed a Cherokee soldier by the name of Jake Awahili had migrated to Virginia after the war. Jack held onto the tin cup for its potential value.

As I continued to read, the town's attorney at the time in 1941 kept Jack's letter, per his request, on file in a sealed envelope and separated it from his will until his death. Jack didn't want anyone to know about the gravesite, the tin cup, or the soldier to whom it belonged. Even Victoria didn't know. It was his secret.

When Jack died, the town's attorney in 1999 read the letter and went to the house to obtain the tin cup. He wasn't able to find it and thought it sold at the estate sale. He wrote a note to this effect and attached it to the letter before he archived it. This note was in the glass case alongside Jack's letter in the museum.

In 2020, Ayesha found out about this archived letter from the town's attorney. It went to the preservation society as part of the sell. Ayesha never read it but was told it was related to a historical artifact found on the property and shared that with Brock and me.

We thought the letter referred to the grenade King found, not the tin cup.

Jack's spirit remained inside our house and knew the tin cup was a personal connection to my family's military past and the gravesite on the property. His letter revealed the tin cup belonged to my third great-grandfather whose grave he covered with his house.

During the excavation, one archaeologist was able to locate the tin cup, which hid in a metal bread box inside the charred bottom stove drawer. How had the tin cup ended up there? The museum was solving that question. But I believed I knew the answer.

In the kitchen on moving day, Jack removed the metal bread box with the tin cup from the sealed box. He placed it back inside the cabinet. He thought of it as his property and no one else could have it.

When I was at the house for the cleansing and Jack choked me, he saw Tori in the bedroom and released me from his death grip. His spirit went back to the kitchen cabinet, took the bread box with the tin cup, and placed it in the stove's bottom drawer for added protection from the fire in the house.

Jack didn't want anyone else to have his possessions, which included his wife, his house, and his tin cup. The tin cup was the only thing left Jack could hold on to. It wouldn't die and leave him as Tori had done. Even the house fire couldn't destroy it.

At that moment, I turned around and noticed the light shining above the tin cup in the glass dome flickered. I could smell a stale cigarette odor which hovered in the air. There was an icy-cold sensation where I stood. A frigid chill ran across my body. The hairs on my arms and back of my neck stood up.

I knew without a doubt where it came from and who was there in the museum. He would never go away as long as the tin cup stayed. It was his tin cup and no one else's. His spirit had an attachment to the tin cup which gave him sustenance and kept him from entering the dark spirit underworld forever. The tin cup he found, not on the museum's property, but on his property eighty-one years ago at 119 Westview Lane . . . JACK.

THE END

AUTHOR NOTE

Dear Reader:

I hope you enjoyed reading my first novel, **_SPIRIT OBSESSED_**. It has been a labor of love and devotion to see this story through from beginning to end.

I have not written a bucket list of things to be accomplished during my lifetime. But I have tried to set one goal at a time for myself and made a promise to never quit until I reached it. Writing a novel has always been one of my personal goals. It's been a privilege to share it with you today.

Again, thank you for the time you spent reading my story and your support in my journey as a new author.

Sincerely,

Brenda Bengtson
www.brendabengtson.com

ACKNOWLEDGEMENTS

First, I would like to thank God for sending his son Jesus into the world to save all who choose to believe in His saving grace and love for us. Next, I would like to thank Chandler Bolt and the Self-Publishing School team for their guidance throughout this fiction book process. I could not have achieved my dream of writing this book without your support. A heartfelt thanks to my coaches Ramy Vance and Barbara Hartzler.

I would like to extend my gratitude to my wonderful editor, Rachel Garber, for her expert guidance, the staff at Cutting-Edge Studio book cover designer Marijke van Leeuwen, book description guidance Joris van Leeuwen, and formatter for their expertise in preparing this book for publication. You are awesome!

I would also like to thank my husband, Bob, for his love and support throughout my journey. You are my rock!

Also, thank you to the launch team for your steadfast support. You are amazing!

I would like to give a big shout out to all the baristas at Starbucks and BNN in Roanoke, Virginia for the endless supply of Venti Peppermint Mochas to keep my brain pumped while writing. You're the best!

Finally, I would like to acknowledge my parents Arthur and Mary (love you Mom and Dad). My father was my writing mentor. As a child, I watched him write every day at the kitchen table in his green notebook with a dream of publishing a story one day. Rest in peace Dad. This one's for you.

ABOUT THE AUTHOR

Brenda Bengtson is a wife, mother, and registered nurse from Roanoke, Virginia. Stories about near death situations with God's intervention and haunted houses with unexplained paranormal activity have always piqued her interest. When her own family had an unexpected experience with a spirit encounter, it led to her first fiction novel *Spirit Obsessed*. Aside from writing, she enjoys learning new things to keep her brain young and relaxing with a cup of peppermint mocha coffee without any ghostly interruptions.

CAN YOU HELP?

"Thank You For Reading My Grandma's Book!"

Dear Reader:

Please leave me an honest review wherever you purchased this book.

Thank you for reading **SPIRIT OBSESSED.**

Brenda Bengtson

www.brendabengtson.com

Self-Publishing School

N OW IT'S YOUR TURN

Discover the EXACT 3-step blueprint you need to become a bestselling author in as little as 3 months.

Self-Publishing School helped me, and now I want them to help you with this FREE resource to begin outlining your book!

Even if you're busy, bad at writing, or don't know where to start,

you CAN write a bestseller and build your best life.

With tools and experience across a variety of niches and professions,

Self-Publishing School is the only resource you need to

take your book to the finish line!

DON'T WAIT

Say "YES" to becoming a bestseller

https://self-publishingschool.com/friend/

Follow the steps on the page to get a FREE resource to get started on your book and unlock a discount to get started with Self-Publishing School